Shorter Poems

Shorter Poems

by

Robert Browning

CAMBRIDGE
SCHOLARS
PUBLISHING

classic texts

Shorter Poems, by Robert Browning

This book in its current typographical format first published 2008 by

Cambridge Scholars Publishing

12 Back Chapman Street, Newcastle upon Tyne, NE6 2XX, UK

British Library Cataloguing in Publication Data
A catalogue record for this book is available from the British Library

ISBN (10): 1-4438-0062-7, ISBN (13): 978-1-4438-0062-4

CONTENTS

THE PIED PIPER OF HAMELIN 1

TRAY 14

INCIDENT OF THE FRENCH CAMP 16

"HOW THEY BROUGHT THE GOOD NEWS FROM GHENT TO AIX" 19

HERVÉ RIEL 23

PHEIDIPPIDES 30

MY STAR 36

EVELYN HOPE 37

LOVE AMONG THE RUINS 40

MISCONCEPTIONS 44

NATURAL MAGIC 45

APPARITIONS 46

A WALL 47

CONFESSIONS 49

A WOMAN'S LAST WORD 52

A PRETTY WOMAN 55

YOUTH AND ART 60

A TALE 65

CAVALIER TUNES 71

I. MARCHING ALONG *71*

II. GIVE A ROUSE *72*

III. BOOT AND SADDLE *74*

HOME-THOUGHTS, FROM THE SEA 76

SUMMUM BONUM 77

A FACE 78

SONGS FROM 'PIPPA PASSES' 79

THE LOST LEADER 82

APPARENT FAILURE 84

FEARS AND SCRUPLES 88

INSTANS TYRANNUS 91

THE PATRIOT 95

THE BOY AND THE ANGEL 97

MEMORABILIA 101

WHY I AM A LIBERAL 102

PROSPICE 103

EPILOGUE TO "ASOLANDO" 105

"DE GUSTIBUS—" 106

THE ITALIAN IN ENGLAND 108

MY LAST DUCHESS 114

THE BISHOP ORDERS HIS TOMB AT SAINT PRAXED'S CHURCH 117

THE LABORATORY 122

HOME THOUGHTS, FROM ABROAD 126

UP AT A VILLA—DOWN IN THE CITY 127

A TOCCATA OF GALUPPI'S 131

ABT VOGLER 135

RABBI BEN EZRA 140

A GRAMMARIAN'S FUNERAL 151

ANDREA DEL SARTO 157

CALIBAN UPON SETEBOS 167

"CHILDE ROLAND TO THE DARK TOWER CAME" 178

AN EPISTLE 190

SAUL 202

ONE WORD MORE 217

THE PIED PIPER OF HAMELIN

A CHILD'S STORY

(Written for, and inscribed to W. M. the Younger)

I

Hamelin town's in Brunswick,
By famous Hanover city;
The river Weser, deep and wide,
Washes its walls on either side;
A pleasanter spot you never spied;
But, when begins my ditty,
Almost five hundred years ago,
To see the townsfolk suffer so
From vermin, was a pity.

II

Rats!
They fought the dogs and killed the cats,
And bit the babies in the cradles,
And ate the cheeses out of the vats,
And licked the soup from the cooks' own ladles,
Split open the kegs of salted sprats.
Made nests inside men's Sunday hats.

And even spoiled the women's chats
    By drowning their speaking
    With shrieking and squeaking
In fifty different sharps and flats.

III

At last the people in a body
    To the Town Hall came flocking:
"'Tis clear," cried they, "our Mayor's a noddy;
    And as for our Corporation, shocking
To think we buy gowns lined with ermine
For dolts that can't or won't determine
What's best to rid us of our vermin!
You hope, because you're old and obese,
To find in the furry civic robe ease!
Rouse up, sirs! give your brains a racking
To find the remedy we're lacking,
Or, sure as fate, we'll send you packing!"
At this the Mayor and Corporation
Quaked with a mighty consternation.

IV

An hour they sat in council;
    At length the Mayor broke silence:
"For a guilder I'd my ermine gown sell,
I wish I were a mile hence!
It's easy to bid one rack one's brain—

I'm sure my poor head aches again
I've scratched it so, and all in vain.
Oh for a trap, a trap, a trap!"
Just as he said this, what should hap
At the chamber door but a gentle tap?
"Bless us," cried the Mayor, "what's that?"
(With the Corporation as he sat,
Looking little, though wondrous fat;
Nor brighter was his eye, nor moister
Than a too-long-opened oyster,
Save when at noon his paunch grew mutinous
For a plate of turtle, green and glutinous)
"Only a scraping of shoes on the mat?
Anything like the sound of a rat
Makes my heart go pit-a-pat!"

V

"Come in!"—the Mayor cried, looking bigger:
And in did come the strangest figure!
His queer long coat from heel to head
Was half of yellow and half of red,
And he himself was tall and thin,
With sharp blue eyes, each like a pin,
With light loose hair, yet swarthy skin,
No tuft on cheek, nor beard on chin,
But lips where smiles went out and in;
There was no guessing his kith and kin:
And nobody could enough admire

The tall man and his quaint attire.
Quoth one: "It's as my great grandsire,
Starting up at the Trump of Doom's tone,
Had walked his way from his painted tombstone!"

VI

He advanced to the council-table:
And, "Please your honors," said he, "I'm able,
By means of a secret charm, to draw
    All creatures living beneath the sun,
    That creep or swim or fly or run,
After me so as you never saw!
And I chiefly use my charm
On creatures that do people harm,
The mole and toad and newt and viper;
And people call me the Pied Piper."
(And here they noticed round his neck
    A scarf of red and yellow stripe,
To match with his coat of self-same cheque:
    And at the scarf's end hung a pipe;
And his fingers, they noticed, were ever straying,
As if impatient to be playing
Upon this pipe, as low it dangled
Over his vesture so old-fangled.)
"Yet," said he, "poor piper as I am,
In Tartary I freed the Cham,
Last June, from his huge swarms of gnats;
I eased in Asia the Nizam

Of a monstrous brood of vampire-bats:
And as for what your brain bewilders,
If I can rid your town of rats
Will you give me a thousand guilders?"
"One? fifty thousand!"—was the exclamation
Of the astonished Mayor and Corporation.

VII

Into the street the Piper stept,
Smiling first a little smile,
As if he knew what magic slept
In his quiet pipe the while:
Then, like a musical adept,
To blow the pipe his lips he wrinkled,
And green and blue his sharp eyes twinkled,
Like a candle-flame where salt is sprinkled;
And ere three shrill notes the pipe uttered,
You heard as if an army muttered:
And the muttering grew to a grumbling;
And the grumbling grew to a mighty rumbling;
And out of the houses the rats came tumbling.
Great rats, small rats, lean rats, brawny rats,
Brown rats, black rats, gray rats, tawny rats,
Grave old plodders, gay young friskers,
Fathers, mothers, uncles, cousins,
Cocking tails and pricking whiskers,
Families by tens and dozens,
Brothers, sisters, husbands, wives—

Followed the Piper for their lives.
From street to street he piped advancing,
And step for step they followed dancing,
Until they came to the river Weser,
    Wherein all plunged and perished!
—Save one, who, stout as Julius Caesar,
Swam across and lived to carry
    (As he, the manuscript he cherished)
To Rat-land home his commentary:
Which was: "At the first shrill notes of the pipe,
I heard a sound as of scraping tripe,
And putting apples, wondrous ripe,
Into a cider press's gripe;
And a moving away of pickle-tub-boards,
And a leaving ajar of conserve-cupboards,
And a drawing the corks of train-oil-flasks,
And a breaking the hoops of butter-casks:
And it seemed as if a voice
    (Sweeter far than by harp or by psaltery
Is breathed) called out, 'Oh, rats, rejoice!
The world is grown to one vast drysaltery!
So munch on, crunch on, take your nuncheon,
Breakfast, supper, dinner, luncheon!'
And just as a bulky sugar-puncheon,
Already staved, like a great sun shone
Glorious scarce an inch before me,
Just as methought it said, 'Come, bore me!'
—I found the Weser rolling o'er me."

VIII

You should have heard the Hamelin people
Ringing the bells till they rocked the steeple.
"Go," cried the Mayor, "and get long poles,
Poke out the nests and block up the holes!
Consult with carpenters and builders,
And leave in our town, not even a trace
Of the rats!"—when suddenly, up the face
Of the Piper perked in the market-place,
With a, "First, if you please, my thousand guilders!"

IX

A thousand guilders! The Mayor looked blue;
So did the Corporation, too.
For council dinners made rare havoc
With Claret, Moselle, in-de-Grave, Hock;
And half the money would replenish
Their cellar's biggest butt with Rhenish.
To pay this sum to a wandering fellow
With a gypsy coat of red and yellow!
"Beside," quoth the Mayor, with a knowing wink,
"Our business was done at the river's brink;
We saw with our eyes the vermin sink,
And what's dead can't come to life, I think.
So, friend, we're not the folks to shrink
From the duty of giving you something for drink,
And a matter of money to put in your poke;

But as for the guilders, what we spoke
Of them, as you very well know, was in joke.
Beside, our losses have made us thrifty.
A thousand guilders! Come, take fifty!"

X

The Piper's face fell, and he cried,
"No trifling! I can't wait! Beside,
I've promised to visit by dinner-time
Bagdat, and accept the prime
Of the Head-Cook's pottage, all he's rich in,
For having left, in the Caliph's kitchen,
Of a nest of scorpions no survivor:
With him I proved no bargain-driver,
With you, don't think I'll bate a stiver!
And folks who put me in a passion
May find me pipe after another fashion."

XI

"How?" cried the Mayor, "d'ye think I brook
Being worse treated than a cook?
Insulted by a lazy ribald
With idle pipe and vesture piebald?
You threaten us, fellow? Do your worst!
Blow your pipe there till you burst!"

XII

Once more he stept into the street,
    And to his lips again
Laid his long pipe of smooth straight cane;
And ere he blew three notes (such sweet,
Soft notes as yet musician's cunning
    Never gave the enraptured air)
There was a rustling that seemed like a bustling
Of merry crowds justling at pitching and hustling;
Small feet were pattering, wooden shoes clattering,
Little hands clapping, and little tongues chattering,
And, like fowls in a farm-yard, when barley is scattering,
Out came the children running.
All the little boys and girls.
With rosy cheeks and flaxen curls,
And sparkling eyes and teeth like pearls,
Tripping and skipping, ran merrily after
The wonderful music with shouting and laughter.

XIII

The Mayor was dumb, and the Council stood
As if they were changed into blocks of wood.
Unable to move a step, or cry
To the children merrily skipping by,
—Could only follow with the eye
That joyous crowd at the piper's back.
But how the Mayor was on the rack,

And the wretched Council's bosom beat,
As the Piper turned from the High Street
To where the Weser rolled its waters,
Right in the way of their sons and daughters!
However, he turned from South to West,
And to Koppelberg Hill his steps addressed,
And after him the children pressed:
Great was the joy in every breast.
"He never can cross that mighty top!
He's forced to let the piping drop,
And we shall see our children stop."
When lo, as they reached the mountain-side,
A wondrous portal opened wide,
As if a cavern were suddenly hollowed;
And the Piper advanced, and the children followed,
And when all were in, to the very last,
The door in the mountain-side shut fast.
Did I say all? No! One was lame,
    And could not dance the whole of the way;
And in after years, if you would blame
    His sadness, he was used to say,—
"It's dull in our town since my playmates left!
I can't forget that I'm bereft
Of all the pleasant sights they see,
Which the Piper also promised me.
For he led us, he said, to a joyous land.
Joining the town, and just at hand,
Where waters gushed and fruit-trees grew,
And flowers put forth a fairer hue,

And everything was strange and new:
The sparrows were brighter than peacocks here,
And their dogs outran our fallow deer.
And honey-bees had lost their stings,
And horses were born with eagles' wings;
And just as I became assured,
My lame foot would be speedily cured,
The music stopped and I stood still,
And found myself outside the hill,
Left alone against my will,
To go now limping as before.
And never hear of that country more!"

XIV

Alas, alas for Hamelin!
    There came into many a burgher's pate
    A text which says that Heaven's gate
    Opes to the rich at as easy a rate
As the needle's eye takes a camel in!
The Mayor sent East, West, North, and South,
To offer the Piper, by word of mouth,
    Wherever it was men's lot to find him,
Silver and gold to his heart's content,
If he'd only return the way he went,
    And bring the children behind him.
But when they saw 'twas a lost endeavor,
And Piper and dancers were gone forever,
They made a decree that lawyers never

Should think their records dated duly
If, after the day of the month and year,
These words did not as well appear,
"And so long after what happened here
On the twenty-second of July,
Thirteen hundred and seventy-six;"
And the better in memory to fix
The place of the children's last retreat,
They called it the Pied Piper's Street—
Where any one playing on pipe or tabor
Was sure for the future to lose his labour.
Nor suffered they hostelry or tavern
To shock with mirth a street so solemn;
But opposite the place of the cavern
They wrote the story on a column,
And on the great church window painted
The same, to make the world acquainted
How their children were stolen away.
And there it stands to this very day.
And I must not omit to say
That in Transylvania there's a tribe
Of alien people who ascribe
The outlandish ways and dress
On which their neighbours lay such stress,
To their fathers and mothers having risen
Out of some subterraneous prison

Into which they were trepanned
Long time ago in a mighty band
Out of Hamelin town in Brunswick land,
But how or why, they don't understand.

XV

So, Willy, let me and you be wipers
Of scores out with all men—especially pipers!
And, whether they pipe us free from rats or from mice,
If we've promised them aught, let us keep our promise!

TRAY

Sing me a hero! Quench my thirst
Of soul, ye bards!
                                        Quoth Bard the first:
"Sir Olaf, the good knight, did don
His helm, and eke his habergeon..."
Sir Olaf and his bard—!

"That sin-scathed brow" (quoth Bard the second),
"That eye wide ope as tho' Fate beckoned
My hero to some steep, beneath
Which precipice smiled tempting Death..."
You too without your host have reckoned!

"A beggar-child" (let's hear this third!)
"Sat on a quay's edge: like a bird
Sang to herself at careless play,
And fell into the stream. 'Dismay!
Help, you the standers-by!' None stirred.

"Bystanders reason, think of wives
And children ere they risk their lives.
Over the balustrade has bounced
A mere instinctive dog, and pounced
Plumb on the prize. 'How well he dives!

"'Up he comes with the child, see, tight
In mouth, alive too, clutched from quite
A depth of ten feet—twelve, I bet!
Good dog! What, off again? There's yet
Another child to save? All right!

"'How strange we saw no other fall!
It's instinct in the animal.
Good dog! But he's a long while under:
If he got drowned I should not wonder—
Strong current, that against the wall!

"'Here he comes, holds in mouth this time
—What may the thing be? Well, that's prime!
Now, did you ever? Reason reigns
In man alone, since all Tray's pains
Have fished—the child's doll from the slime!'

"And so, amid the laughter gay,
Trotted my hero off,—old Tray,—
Till somebody, prerogatived
With reason, reasoned: 'Why he dived,
His brain would show us, I should say.

"'John, go and catch—or, if needs be,
Purchase that animal for me!
By vivisection, at expense
Of half-an-hour and eighteen pence,
How brain secretes dog's soul, we'll see!'"

INCIDENT OF THE FRENCH CAMP

I

You know, we French stormed Ratisbon:
    A mile or so away
On a little mound, Napoleon
    Stood on our storming-day;
With neck out-thrust, you fancy how,
    Legs wide, arms locked behind,
As if to balance the prone brow
    Oppressive with its mind.

II

Just as perhaps he mused "My plans
    That soar, to earth may fall,
Let once my army-leader Lannes
    Waver at yonder wall"—
Out 'twixt the battery-smokes there flew
    A rider, bound on bound
Full-galloping; nor bridle drew
    Until he reached the mound,

III

Then off there flung in smiling joy,
    And held himself erect
By just his horse's mane, a boy:
    You hardly could suspect—
(So tight he kept his lips compressed.
    Scarce any blood came through)
You looked twice ere you saw his breast
    Was all but shot in two.

IV

"Well," cried he, "Emperor, by God's grace
    We've got you Ratisbon!
The Marshal's in the market-place,
    And you'll be there anon
To see your flag-bird flap his vans
    Where I, to heart's desire,
Perched him!" The chief's eye flashed; his plans
    Soared up again like fire.

V

The chief's eye flashed; but presently
    Softened itself, as sheathes
A film the mother-eagle's eye
    When her bruised eaglet breathes.

"You're wounded!" "Nay," the soldier's pride
    Touched to the quick, he said:
"I'm killed, Sire!" And his chief beside,
    Smiling, the boy fell dead.

"HOW THEY BROUGHT THE GOOD NEWS FROM GHENT TO AIX"

[16—]

I

I sprang to the stirrup, and Joris, and he;

I galloped, Dirck galloped, we galloped all three;

"Good speed!" cried the watch, as the gate-bolts undrew;

"Speed!" echoed the wall to us galloping through;

Behind shut the postern, the lights sank to rest,

And into the midnight we galloped abreast.

II

Not a word to each other; we kept the great pace

Neck by neck, stride by stride, never changing our place;

I turned in my saddle and made its girths tight,

Then shortened each stirrup, and set the pique right,

Rebuckled the cheek-strap, chained slacker the bit,

Nor galloped less steadily Roland a whit.

III

'Twas moonset at starting; but while we drew near
Lokeren, the cocks crew and twilight dawned clear:
At Boom, a great yellow star came out to see;
At Dueffeld, 'twas morning as plain as could be;
And from Mecheln church-steeple we heard the half-chime,
So, Joris broke silence with, "Yet there is time!"

IV

At Aershot up leaped of a sudden the sun,
And against him the cattle stood black every one,
To stare through the mist at us galloping past,
And I saw my stout galloper Roland, at last,
With resolute shoulders, each butting away
The haze, as some bluff river headland its spray:

V

And his low head and crest, just one sharp ear bent back
For my voice, and the other pricked out on his track;
And one eye's black intelligence,—ever that glance
O'er its white edge at me, his own master, askance!
And the thick heavy spume-flakes which aye and anon
His fierce lips shook upwards in galloping on.

VI

By Hasselt, Dirck groaned; and cried Joris, "Stay spur!
Your Roos galloped bravely, the fault's not in her,
We'll remember at Aix"—for one heard the quick wheeze
Of her chest, saw the stretched neck and staggering knees,
And sunk tail, and horrible heave of the flank,
As down on her haunches she shuddered and sank.

VII

So, we were left galloping, Joris and I,
Past Looz and past Tongres, no cloud in the sky;
The broad sun above laughed a pitiless laugh,
'Neath our feet broke the brittle bright stubble like chaff;
Till over by Dalhem a dome-spire sprang white,
And "Gallop," gasped Joris, "for Aix is in sight!"

VIII

"How they'll greet us!"—and all in a moment his roan
Rolled neck and croup over, lay dead as a stone;
And there was my Roland to bear the whole weight
Of the news which alone could save Aix from her fate,
With his nostrils like pits full of blood to the brim,
And with circles of red for his eye-sockets' rim.

IX

Then I cast loose my buff-coat, each holster let fall,
Shook off both my jack-boots, let go belt and all,
Stood up in the stirrup, leaned, patted his ear,
Called my Roland his pet-name, my horse without peer;
Clapped my hands, laughed and sang, any noise, bad or good,
Till at length, into Aix Roland galloped and stood.

X

And all I remember is,—friends flocking round
As I sat with his head 'twixt my knees on the ground;
And no voice but was praising this Roland of mine,
As I poured down his throat our last measure of wine,
Which (the burgesses voted by common consent)
Was no more than his due who brought good news from Ghent.

HERVÉ RIEL

I

On the sea and at the Hogue, sixteen hundred ninety two,
    Did the English fight the French,—woe to France!
And, the thirty-first of May, helter-skelter thro' the blue.
Like a crowd of frightened porpoises a shoal of sharks pursue,
    Came crowding ship on ship to St. Malo on the Rance,
With the English fleet in view.

II

'Twas the squadron that escaped, with the victor in full chase;
    First and foremost of the drove, in his great ship, Damfreville;
        Close on him fled, great and small,
    Twenty-two good ships in all;
And they signalled to the place
"Help the winners of a race!
    Get us guidance, give us harbor, take us quick—or, quicker still,
    Here's the English can and will!"

III

Then the pilots of the place put out brisk and leapt on board;
    "Why, what hope or chance have ships like these to pass?" laughed they:
"Rocks to starboard, rocks to port, all the passage scarred and scored,
Shall the '*Formidable*' here, with her twelve and eighty guns

Think to make the river-mouth by the single narrow way,
Trust to enter where 'tis ticklish for a craft of twenty tons,
And with flow at full beside?
Now 'tis slackest ebb of tide.
Reach the mooring? Rather say,
While rock stands or water runs,
Not a ship will leave the bay!"

IV

Then was called a council straight.
Brief and bitter the debate:
"Here's the English at our heels; would you have them take in tow
All that's left us of the fleet, linked together stern and bow,
For a prize to Plymouth Sound?
Better run the ships aground!"
(Ended Damfreville his speech).
Not a minute more to wait!
"Let the Captains all and each
Shove ashore, then blow up, burn the vessels on the beach!
France must undergo her fate.

V

"Give the word!" But no such word
Was ever spoke or heard;
For up stood, for out stepped, for in struck amid all these
—A Captain? A Lieutenant? A Mate—first, second, third?

No such man of mark, and meet
With his betters to compete!
But a simple Breton sailor pressed by Tourville for the fleet,
A poor coasting-pilot he, Hervé Riel the Croisickese.

VI

And, "What mockery or malice have we here?" cries Hervé Riel:
"Are you mad, you Malouins? Are you cowards, fools, or rogues?
Talk to me of rocks and shoals, me who took the soundings, tell
On my fingers every bank, every shallow, every swell
'Twixt the offing here and Grève where the river disembogues?
Are you bought by English gold? Is it love the lying's for?
Morn and eve, night and day,
Have I piloted your bay,
Entered free and anchored fast at the foot of Solidor.
Burn the fleet and ruin France? That were worse than fifty Hogues!
Sirs, they know I speak the truth! Sirs, believe me there's a way!
Only let me lead the line,
Have the biggest ship to steer,
Get this '*Formidable*' clear,
Make the others follow mine,
And I lead them, most and least, by a passage I know well,
Right to Solidor past Greve,
And there lay them safe and sound;
And if one ship misbehave,
—Keel so much as grate the ground.
Why, I've nothing but my life,—here's my head!" cries Hervé Riel.

VII

Not a minute more to wait.
"Steer us in then, small and great!
    Take the helm, lead the line, save the squadron!" cried its chief.
Captains, give the sailor place!
    He is Admiral, in brief.
Still the north-wind, by God's grace!
See the noble fellow's face
As the big ship, with a bound,
Clears the entry like a hound,
Keeps the passage as its inch of way were the wide sea's profound!
    See, safe thro' shoal and rock,
    How they follow in a flock,
Not a ship that misbehaves, not a keel that grates the ground,
    Not a spar that comes to grief!
The peril, see, is past,
All are harboured to the last,
And just as Hervé Riel hollas "Anchor!"—sure as fate
Up the English come,—too late!

VIII

So, the storm subsides to calm:
    They see the green trees wave
    On the heights o'erlooking Grève.
Hearts that bled are staunched with balm.
"Just our rapture to enhance,
    Let the English rake the bay,

Gnash their teeth and glare askance
    As they cannonade away!
'Neath rampired Solidor pleasant riding on the Rance!"
How hope succeeds despair on each Captain's countenance!
Out burst all with one accord,
    "This is Paradise for Hell!
        Let France, let France's King
        Thank the man that did the thing!"
What a shout, and all one word,
    "Hervé Riel!"
As he stepped in front once more,
    Not a symptom of surprise
    In the frank blue Breton eyes,
Just the same man as before.

IX

Then said Damfreville, "My friend,
I must speak out at the end,
    Tho' I find the speaking hard.
Praise is deeper than the lips:
You have saved the King his ships,
    You must name your own reward,
'Faith our sun was near eclipse!
Demand whate'er you will,
France remains your debtor still.
Ask to heart's content and have! or my name's not Damfreville."

X

Then a beam of fun outbroke
On the bearded mouth that spoke,
As the honest heart laughed through
Those frank eyes of Breton blue:
"Since I needs must say my say,
    Since on board the duty's done,
    And from Malo Roads to Croisic Point, what is it but a run?—
Since 'tis ask and have, I may—
    Since the others go ashore—
Come! A good whole holiday!
    Leave to go and see my wife, whom I call the Belle Aurore!"
    That he asked and that he got,—nothing more.

XI

Name and deed alike are lost:
Not a pillar nor a post
    In his Croisic keeps alive the feat as it befell;
Not a head in white and black
On a single fishing smack,
In memory of the man but for whom had gone to wrack
    All that France saved from the fight whence England bore the bell.
Go to Paris: rank on rank.
    Search the heroes flung pell-mell
On the Louvre, face and flank!
    You shall look long enough ere you come to Hervé Riel.

So, for better and for worse,

Hervé Riel, accept my verse!

In my verse, Hervé Riel, do thou once more

Save the squadron, honour France, love thy wife the Belle Aurore!

PHEIDIPPIDES

Χαίρετε, νικώμεν

First I salute this soil of the blessed, river and rock!
Gods of my birthplace, daemons and heroes, honour to all!
Then I name thee, claim thee for our patron, co-equal in praise
—Ay, with Zeus the Defender, with Her of the aegis and spear!
Also, ye of the bow and the buskin, praised be your peer,
Now, henceforth, and forever,—O latest to whom I upraise
Hand and heart and voice! For Athens, leave pasture and flock!
Present to help, potent to save, Pan—patron I call!

Archons of Athens, topped by the tettix, see, I return!
See, 'tis myself here standing alive, no spectre that speaks!
Crowned with the myrtle, did you command me, Athens and you,
"Run, Pheidippides, run and race, reach Sparta for aid!
Persia has come, we are here, where is She?" Your command I obeyed,
Ran and raced: like stubble, some field which a fire runs through,
Was the space between city and city: two days, two nights did I burn
Over the hills, under the dales, down pits and up peaks.

Into their midst I broke: breath served but for "Persia has come!
Persia bids Athens proffer slaves'-tribute, water and earth
Razed to the ground is Eretria—but Athens, shall Athens sink,
Drop into dust and die—the flower of Hellas utterly die,

Die with the wide world spitting at Sparta, the stupid, the stander-by?
Answer me quick,—what help, what hand do you stretch o'er destruction's brink?
How,—when? No care for my limbs!—there's lightning in all and some—
Fresh and fit your message to bear, once lips give it birth!"

O my Athens—Sparta love thee? did Sparta respond?
Every face of her leered in a furrow of envy, mistrust,
Malice,—each eye of her gave me its glitter of gratified hate!
Gravely they turned to take counsel, to cast for excuses. I stood
Quivering,—the limbs of me fretting as fire frets, an inch from dry wood:
"Persia has come, Athens asks aid, and still they debate?
Thunder, thou Zeus! Athene, are Spartans a quarry beyond
Swing of thy spear? Phoibos and Artemis, clang them 'Ye must'!"

No bolt launched from Olumpos! Lo, their answer at last!
"Has Persia come,—does Athens ask aid,—may Sparta befriend?
Nowise precipitate judgment—too weighty the issue at stake!
Count we no time lost time which lags thro' respect to the Gods!
Ponder that precept of old, 'No warfare, whatever the odds
In your favour, so long as the moon, half-orbed, is unable to take
Full-circle her state in the sky!' Already she rounds to it fast:
Athens must wait, patient as we—who judgment suspend."

Athens,—except for that sparkle,—thy name, I had mouldered to ash!
That sent a blaze thro' my blood; off, off and away was I back,
—Not one word to waste, one look to lose on the false and the vile!
Yet "O Gods of my land!" I cried, as each hillock and plain,

Wood and stream, I knew, I named, rushing past them again,
"Have ye kept faith, proved mindful of honours we paid you erewhile?
Vain was the filleted victim, the fulsome libation! Too rash
Love in its choice, paid you so largely service so slack!

"Oak and olive and bay,—I bid you cease to en-wreathe
Brows made bold by your leaf! Fade at the Persian's foot,
You that, our patrons were pledged, should never adorn a slave!
Rather I hail thee, Parnes,—trust to thy wild waste tract!
Treeless, herbless, lifeless mountain! What matter if slacked
My speed may hardly be, for homage to crag and to cave
No deity deigns to drape with verdure?—at least I can breathe,
Fear in thee no fraud from the blind, no lie from the mute!"

Such my cry as, rapid, I ran over Parnes' ridge;
Gully and gap I clambered and cleared till, sudden, a bar
Jutted, a stoppage of stone against me, blocking the way.
Right! for I minded the hollow to traverse, the fissure across:
"Where I could enter, there I depart by! Night in the fosse?
Athens to aid? Tho' the dive were thro' Erebos, thus I obey—
Out of the day dive, into the day as bravely arise! No bridge
Better!"—when—ha! what was it I came on, of wonders that are?

There, in the cool of a cleft, sat he—majestical Pan!
Ivy drooped wanton, kissed his head, moss cushioned his hoof;
All the great God was good in the eyes grave-kindly—the curl
Carved on the bearded cheek, amused at a mortal's awe

As, under the human trunk, the goat-thighs grand I saw.
"Halt, Pheidippides!"—halt I did, my brain of a whirl:
"Hither to me! Why pale in my presence?" he gracious began:
"How is it,—Athens, only in Hellas, holds me aloof?

"Athens, she only, rears me no fane, makes me no feast!
Wherefore? Than I what godship to Athens more helpful of old?
Ay, and still, and forever her friend! Test Pan, trust me!
Go bid Athens take heart, laugh Persia to scorn, have faith
In the temples and tombs! Go, say to Athens, 'The Goat-God saith:
When Persia—so much as strews not the soil—Is cast in the sea,
Then praise Pan who fought in the ranks with your most and least,
Goat-thigh to greaved-thigh, made one cause with the free and the bold!'

"Say Pan saith: 'Let this, foreshowing the place, be the pledge!'"
(Gay, the liberal hand held out this herbage I bear
—Fennel,—I grasped it a-tremble with dew—whatever it bode),
"While, as for thee..." But enough! He was gone. If I ran hitherto—
Be sure that the rest of my journey, I ran no longer, but flew.
Parnes to Athens—earth no more, the air was my road;
Here am I back. Praise Pan, we stand no more on the razor's edge!
Pan for Athens, Pan for me! I too have a guerdon rare!

* * * * *

Then spoke Miltiades. "And thee, best runner of Greece,
Whose limbs did duty indeed,—what gift is promised thyself?
Tell it us straightway,—Athens the mother demands of her son!"
Rosily blushed the youth: he paused: but, lifting at length

His eyes from the ground, it seemed as he gathered the rest of his strength
Into the utterance—"Pan spoke thus: 'For what thou hast done
Count on a worthy reward! Henceforth be allowed thee release
From the racer's toil, no vulgar reward in praise or in pelf!'

"I am bold to believe, Pan means reward the most to my mind!
Fight I shall, with our foremost, wherever this fennel may grow,—
Pound—Pan helping us—Persia to dust, and, under the deep,
Whelm her away forever; and then,—no Athens to save,—
Marry a certain maid, I know keeps faith to the brave,—
Hie to my house and home: and, when my children shall creep
Close to my knees,—recount how the God was awful yet kind,
Promised their sire reward to the full—rewarding him—so!"

* * * * *

Unforeseeing one! Yes, he fought on the Marathon day:
So, when Persia was dust, all cried "To Akropolis!
Run, Pheidippides, one race more! the meed is thy due!
'Athens is saved, thank Pan,' go shout!" He flung down his shield,
Ran like fire once more: and the space 'twixt the Fennel-field
And Athens was stubble again, a field which a fire runs through,
Till in he broke: "Rejoice, we conquer!" Like wine thro' clay,
Joy in his blood bursting his heart, he died—the bliss!

So, to this day, when friend meets friend, the word of salute
Is still "Rejoice!"—his word which brought rejoicing indeed.
So is Pheidippides happy forever,—the noble strong man
Who could race like a god, bear the face of a god, whom a god loved so well,
He saw the land saved he had helped to save, and was suffered to tell
Such tidings, yet never decline, but, gloriously as he began,
So to end gloriously—once to shout, thereafter be mute:
"Athens is saved!"—Pheidippides dies in the shout for his meed.

MY STAR

All that I know
    Of a certain star
Is, it can throw
    (Like the angled spar)
Now a dart of red,
    Now a dart of blue;
Till my friends have said
    They would fain see, too,
My star that dartles the red and the blue!

Then it stops like a bird; like a flower, hangs furled:
    They must solace themselves with the Saturn above it.
What matter to me if their star is a world?
    Mine has opened its soul to me; therefore I love it.

EVELYN HOPE

I

Beautiful Evelyn Hope is dead!
Sit and watch by her side an hour.
That is her book-shelf, this her bed;
She plucked that piece of geranium-flower,
Beginning to die too, in the glass;
Little has yet been changed, I think:
The shutters are shut, no light may pass
Save two long rays thro' the hinge's chink.

II

Sixteen years old when she died!
Perhaps she had scarcely heard my name;
It was not her time to love; beside,
Her life had many a hope and aim,
Duties enough and little cares,
And now was quiet, now astir,
Till God's hand beckoned unawares,—
And the sweet white brow is all of her.

III

Is it too late then, Evelyn Hope?
    What, your soul was pure and true,
The good stars met in your horoscope,
    Made you of spirit, fire and dew—
And just because I was thrice as old
    And our paths in the world diverged so wide,
Each was naught to each, must I be told?
    We were fellow mortals, nought beside?

IV

No, indeed! for God above
    Is great to grant, as mighty to make,
And creates the love to reward the love:
    I claim you still, for my own love's sake!
Delayed it may be for more lives yet,
    Thro' worlds I shall traverse, not a few:
Much is to learn, much, to forget
    Ere the time be come for taking you.

V

But the time will come, at last it will,
    When, Evelyn Hope, what meant (I shall say)
In the lower earth in the years long still,
    That body and soul so pure and gay?

Why your hair was amber, I shall divine,
    And your mouth of your own geranium's red—
And what would you do with me, in fine,
    In the new life come in the old one's stead.

VI

I have lived (I shall say) so much since then,
    Given up myself so many times,
Gained me the gains of various men,
    Ransacked the ages, spoiled the climes;
Yet one thing, one, in my soul's full scope,
    Either I missed or itself missed me:
And I want and find you, Evelyn Hope!
    What is the issue? let us see!

VII

I loved you, Evelyn, all the while!
    My heart seemed full as it could hold;
There was place and to spare for the frank young smile,
    And the red young mouth, and the hair's young gold.
So hush,—I will give you this leaf to keep:
    See, I shut it inside the sweet cold hand!
There, that is our secret: go to sleep!
    You will wake, and remember, and understand.

LOVE AMONG THE RUINS

I

Where the quiet-coloured end of evening smiles
    Miles and miles
On the solitary pastures where our sheep
    Half-asleep
Tinkle homeward thro' the twilight, stray or stop
    As they crop—
Was the site once of a city great and gay,
    (So they say)
Of our country's very capital, its prince
    Ages since
Held his court in, gathered councils, wielding far
    Peace or war.

II

Now,—the country does not even boast a tree,
    As you see,
To distinguish slopes of verdure, certain rills
    From the hills
Intersect and give a name to (else they run
    Into one),
Where the domed and daring palace shot its spires
    Up like fires

O'er the hundred-gated circuit of a wall
Bounding all,
Made of marble, men might march on nor be pressed,
Twelve abreast.

III

And such plenty and perfection, see, of grass
Never was!
Such a carpet as, this summer-time, o'erspreads
And embeds
Every vestige of the city, guessed alone,
Stock or stone—
Where a multitude of men breathed joy and woe
Long ago;
Lust of glory pricked their hearts up, dread of shame
Struck them tame;
And that glory and that shame alike, the gold
Bought and sold.

IV

Now,—the single little turret that remains
On the plains,
By the caper overrooted, by the gourd
Overscored,
While the patching houseleek's head of blossom winks
Thro' the chinks—

Marks the basement whence a tower in ancient time
        Sprang sublime,
And a burning ring, all round, the chariots traced
        As they raced,
And the monarch and his minions and his dames
        Viewed the games.

V

And I know—while thus the quiet-coloured eve
        Smiles to leave
To their folding, all our many-tinkling fleece
        In such peace,
And the slopes and rills in undistinguished gray
        Melt away—
That a girl with eager eyes and yellow hair
        Waits me there
In the turret whence the charioteers caught soul
        For the goal,
When the king looked, where she looks now, breathless, dumb
        Till I come,

VI

But he looked upon the city, every side,
        Far and wide,
All the mountains topped with temples, all the glades'
        Colonnades,

All the causeys, bridges, aqueducts,—and then,
    All the men!
When I do come, she will speak not, she will stand,
    Either hand
On my shoulder, give her eyes the first embrace
    Of my face,
Ere we rush, ere we extinguish sight and speech
    Each on each.

VII

In one year they sent a million fighters forth
    South and North,
And they built their gods a brazen pillar high
    As the sky,
Yet reserved a thousand chariots in full force—
    Gold, of course.
Oh heart! oh blood that freezes, blood that burns!
    Earth's returns
For whole centuries of folly, noise, and sin!
    Shut them in,
With their triumphs and their glories and the rest!
    Love is best.

MISCONCEPTIONS

I

This is a spray the bird clung to,
Making it blossom with pleasure,
Ere the high tree-top she sprung to,
Fit for her nest and her treasure.
Oh, what a hope beyond measure
Was the poor spray's, which the flying feet hung to,—
So to be singled out, built in, and sung to!

II

This is a heart the Queen leant on,
Thrilled in a minute erratic,
Ere the true bosom she bent on,
Meet for love's regal dalmatic.
Oh, what a fancy ecstatic
Was the poor heart's, ere the wanderer went on—
Love to be saved for it, proffered to, spent on!

NATURAL MAGIC

I

All I can say is—I saw it!
The room was as bare as your hand.
I locked in the swarth little lady,—I swear,
From the head to the foot of her—well, quite as bare!
"No Nautch shall cheat me," said I, "taking my stand
At this bolt which I draw!" And this bolt—I withdraw it,
And there laughs the lady, not bare, but embowered
With—who knows what verdure, o'erfruited, o'erflowered?
Impossible! Only—I saw it!

II

All I can sing is—I feel it!
This life was as blank as that room;
I let you pass in here. Precaution, indeed?
Walls, ceiling, and floor,—not a chance for a weed!
Wide opens the entrance: where's cold, now, where's gloom?
No May to sow seed here, no June to reveal it,
Behold you enshrined in these blooms of your bringing,
These fruits of your bearing—nay, birds of your winging!
A fairy-tale! Only—I feel it!

APPARITIONS

(*Prologue to "The Two Poets of Croisic."*)

I

Such a starved bank of moss
    Till, that May-morn,
Blue ran the flash across:
    Violets were born!

II

Sky—what a scowl of cloud
    Till, near and far,
Ray on ray split the shroud:
    Splendid, a star!

III

World—how it walled about
    Life with disgrace,
Till God's own smile came out:
    That was thy face!

A WALL

(Prologue to Pacchiarotto)

I

O the old wall here! How I could pass
    Life in a long midsummer day,
My feet confined to a plot of grass,
    My eyes from a wall not once away!

II

And lush and lithe do the creepers clothe
    Yon wall I watch, with a wealth of green:
Its bald red bricks draped, nothing loath,
    In lappets of tangle they laugh between.

III

Now, what is it makes pulsate the robe?
    Why tremble the sprays? What life o'erbrims
The body,—the house no eye can probe,—
    Divined, as beneath a robe, the limbs?

IV

And there again! But my heart may guess
    Who tripped behind; and she sang, perhaps:
So the old wall throbbed, and its life's excess
    Died out and away in the leafy wraps.

V

Wall upon wall are between us: life
    And song should away from heart to heart!
I—prison-bird, with a ruddy strife
    At breast, and a lip whence storm-notes start—

VI

Hold on, hope hard in the subtle thing
    That's spirit: tho' cloistered fast, soar free;
Account as wood, brick, stone, this ring
    Of the rueful neighbours, and—forth to thee!

CONFESSIONS

I

What is he buzzing in my ears?
    "Now that I come to die,
Do I view the world as a vale of tears?"
    Ah, reverend sir, not I!

II

What I viewed there once, what I view again
    Where the physic bottles stand
On the table's edge,—is a suburb lane,
    With a wall to my bedside hand.

III

That lane sloped, much as the bottles do,
    From a house you could descry
O'er the garden-wall: is the curtain blue
    Or green to a healthy eye?

IV

To mine, it serves for the old June weather
    Blue above lane and wall;
And that farthest bottle labelled "Ether"
    Is the house o'er-topping all.

V

At a terrace, somewhere near the stopper,
    There watched for me, one June,
A girl: I know, sir, it's improper,
    My poor mind's out of tune.

VI

Only, there was a way...you crept
    Close by the side, to dodge
Eyes in the house, two eyes except:
    They styled their house "The Lodge."

VII

What right had a lounger up their lane?
    But, by creeping very close,
With the good wall's help,—their eyes might strain
    And stretch themselves to Oes,

VIII

Yet never catch her and me together,
    As she left the attic, there,
By the rim of the bottle labelled "Ether,"
    And stole from stair to stair

IX

And stood by the rose-wreathed gate. Alas,
We loved, sir—used to meet;
How sad and bad and mad it was—
But then, how it was sweet!

A WOMAN'S LAST WORD

I

Let's contend no more, Love,
    Strive nor weep:
All be as before, Love,
    —Only sleep!

II

What so wild as words are?
    I and thou
In debate, as birds are,
    Hawk on bough!

III

See the creature stalking
    While we speak!
Hush and hide the talking,
    Cheek on cheek.

IV

What so false as truth is,
    False to thee?
Where the serpent's tooth is,
    Shun the tree—

V

Where the apple reddens,
    Never pry—
Lest we lose our Edens,
    Eve and I.

VI

Be a god and hold me
    With a charm!
Be a man and fold me
    With thine arm!

VII

Teach me, only teach, Love!
    As I ought
I will speak thy speech, Love,
    Think thy thought—

VIII

Meet, if thou require it,
    Both demands,
Laying flesh and spirit
    In thy hands.

IX

That shall be to-morrow,
    Not to-night:
I must bury sorrow
    Out of sight:

X

—Must a little weep, Love,
    (Foolish me!)
And so fall asleep, Love,
    Loved by thee.

A PRETTY WOMAN

I

That fawn-skin-dappled hair of hers,
And the blue eye
Dear and dewy,
And that infantine fresh air of hers!

II

To think men cannot take you, Sweet,
And infold you,
Ay, and hold you,
And so keep you what they make you, Sweet!

III

You like us for a glance, you know—
For a word's sake
Or a sword's sake:
All's the same, whate'er the chance, you know.

IV

And in turn we make you ours, we say—
You and youth too,
Eyes and mouth too,
All the face composed of flowers, we say.

V

All's our own, to make the most of, Sweet—
    Sing and say for,
    Watch and pray for,
Keep a secret or go boast of, Sweet!

VI

But for loving, why, you would not, Sweet,
    Tho' we prayed you,
    Paid you, brayed you
In a mortar—for you could not, Sweet!

VII

So, we leave the sweet face fondly there,
    Be its beauty
    Its sole duty!
Let all hope of grace beyond, lie there!

VIII

And while the face lies quiet there,
    Who shall wonder
    That I ponder
A conclusion? I will try it there.

IX

As,—why must one, for the love foregone
    Scout mere liking?
    Thunder-striking
Earth,—the heaven, we looked above for, gone!

X

Why, with beauty, needs there money be,
    Love with liking?
    Crush the fly-king
In his gauze, because no honey-bee?

XI

May not liking be so simple-sweet,
    If love grew there
    'Twould undo there
All that breaks the cheek to dimples sweet?

XII

Is the creature too imperfect, say?
    Would you mend it
    And so end it?
Since not all addition perfects aye!

XIII

Or is it of its kind, perhaps,
    Just perfection—
    Whence, rejection
Of a grace not to its mind, perhaps?

XIV

Shall we burn up, tread that face at once
    Into tinder,
    And so hinder
Sparks from kindling all the place at once?

XV

Or else kiss away one's soul on her?
    Your love-fancies!
    —A sick man sees
Truer, when his hot eyes roll on her!

XVI

Thus the craftsman thinks to grace the rose,—
    Plucks a mould-flower
    For his gold flower,
Uses fine things that efface the rose.

XVII

Rosy rubies make its cup more rose.
    Precious metals
    Ape the petals,—
Last, some old king locks it up, morose!

XVIII

Then how grace a rose? I know a way!
    Leave it, rather.
    Must you gather?
Smell, kiss, wear it—at last, throw away.

YOUTH AND ART

I

It once might have been, once only:
    We lodged in a street together,
You, a sparrow on the housetop lonely,
    I, a lone she-bird of his feather.

II

Your trade was with sticks and clay,
    You thumbed, thrust, patted, and polished,
Then laughed "They will see some day,
    Smith made, and Gibson demolished."

III

My business was song, song, song;
    I chirped, cheeped, trilled, and twittered,
"Kate Brown's on the boards ere long,
    And Grisi's existence embittered!"

IV

I earned no more by a warble
    Than you by a sketch in plaster;
You wanted a piece of marble,
    I needed a music-master.

V

We studied hard in our styles,
    Chipped each at a crust like Hindoos,
For air, looked out on the tiles,
    For fun, watched each other's windows.

VI

You lounged, like a boy of the South,
    Cap and blouse—nay, a bit of beard too;
Or you got it, rubbing your mouth
    With fingers the clay adhered to.

VII

And I—soon managed to find
    Weak points in the flower-fence facing,
Was forced to put up a blind
    And be safe in my corset-lacing.

VIII

No harm! It was not my fault
    If you never turned your eye's tail up
As I shook upon E *in alt*,
    Or ran the chromatic scale up:

IX

For spring bade the sparrows pair.
    And the boys and girls gave guesses,
And stalls in our street looked rare
    With bulrush and watercresses.

X

Why did not you pinch a flower
    In a pellet of clay and fling it?
Why did not I put a power
    Of thanks in a look or sing it?

XI

I did look, sharp as a lynx,
    (And yet the memory rankles)
When models arrived, some minx
    Tripped up stairs, she and her ankles.

XII

But I think I gave you as good!
    "That foreign fellow,—who can know
How she pays, in a playful mood,
    For his tuning her that piano?"

XIII

Could you say so, and never say
    "Suppose we join hands and fortunes,
And I fetch her from over the way,
    Her, piano, and long tunes and short tunes?"

XIV

No, no: you would not be rash,
    Nor I rasher and something over;
You've to settle yet Gibson's hash,
    And Grisi yet lives in clover.

XV

But you meet the Prince at the Board,
    I'm queen myself at *bals-paré*,
I've married a rich old lord,
    And you're dubbed knight and an R.A.

XVI

Each life unfulfilled, you see;
    It hangs still, patchy and scrappy:
We have not sighed deep, laughed free,
    Starved, feasted, despaired,—been happy

XVII

And nobody calls you a dunce,
    And people suppose me clever;
This could but have happened once,
    And we missed it, lost it forever.

A TALE

(*Epilogue to "The Two Poets of Croisic."*)

I

What a pretty tale you told me
    Once upon a time
—Said you found it somewhere (scold me!)
    Was it prose or was it rhyme,
Greek or Latin? Greek, you said,
While your shoulder propped my head.

II

Anyhow there's no forgetting
    This much if no more,
That a poet (pray, no petting!)
    Yes, a bard, sir, famed of yore,
Went where suchlike used to go,
Singing for a prize, you know.

III

Well, he had to sing, nor merely
    Sing but play the lyre;
Playing was important clearly
    Quite as singing: I desire,
Sir, you keep the fact in mind
For a purpose that's behind.

IV

There stood he, while deep attention
    Held the judges round,
—Judges able, I should mention,
    To detect the slightest sound
Sung or played amiss: such ears
Had old judges, it appears!

V

None the less he sang out boldly,
    Played in time and tune,
Till the judges, weighing coldly
    Each note's worth, seemed, late or soon,
Sure to smile "In vain one tries
Picking faults out: take the prize!"

VI

When, a mischief! Were they seven
    Strings the lyre possessed?
Oh, and afterwards eleven,
    Thank you! Well, sir,—who had guessed
Such ill luck in store?—it happed
One of those same seven strings snapped.

VII

All was lost, then! No! a cricket
    (What "cicada"? Pooh!)
—Some mad thing that left its thicket
    For mere love of music—flew
With its little heart on fire,
Lighted on the crippled lyre.

VIII

So that when (Ah joy!) our singer
    For his truant string
Feels with disconcerted finger,
    What does cricket else but fling
Fiery heart forth, sound the note
Wanted by the throbbing throat?

IX

Ay and, ever to the ending,
    Cricket chirps at need,
Executes the hand's intending,
    Promptly, perfectly,—indeed
Saves the singer from defeat
With her chirrup low and sweet.

X

Till, at ending, all the judges
    Cry with one assent
"Take the prize—a prize who grudges
    Such a voice and instrument?
Why, we took your lyre for harp,
So it shrilled us forth F sharp!"

XI

Did the conqueror spurn the creature
    Once its service done?
That's no such uncommon feature
    In the case when Music's son
Finds his Lotte's power too spent
For aiding soul development.

XII

No! This other, on returning
    Homeward, prize in hand,
Satisfied his bosom's yearning:
    (Sir, I hope you understand!)
—Said "Some record there must be
Of this cricket's help to me!"

XIII

So, he made himself a statue:
    Marble stood, life size;
On the lyre, he pointed at you,
    Perched his partner in the prize;
Never more apart you found
Her, he throned, from him, she crowned.

XIV

That's the tale: its application?
    Somebody I know
Hopes one day for reputation
    Thro' his poetry that's—Oh,
All so learned and so wise
And deserving of a prize!

XV

If he gains one, will some ticket
    When his statue's built,
Tell the gazer "'Twas a cricket
    Helped my crippled lyre, whose lilt
Sweet and low, when strength usurped
Softness' place i'the scale, she chirped?

XVI

"For as victory was nighest,
    While I sang and played,—
With my lyre at lowest, highest,
    Right alike,—one string that made
'Love' sound soft was snapt in twain
Never to be heard again,—

XVII

"Had not a kind cricket fluttered,
    Perched upon the place
Vacant left, and duly uttered
    'Love, Love, Love,' whene'er the bass
Asked the treble to atone
For its somewhat sombre drone."

XVIII

But you don't know music! Wherefore
    Keep on casting pearls
To a—poet? All I care for
    Is—to tell him that a girl's
"Love" comes aptly in when gruff
Grows his singing. (There, enough!)

CAVALIER TUNES

I. MARCHING ALONG

I

Kentish Sir Byng stood for his King,
Bidding the crop-headed Parliament swing:
And, pressing a troop unable to stoop
And see the rogues flourish and honest folk droop,
Marched them along, fifty score strong,
Great-hearted gentlemen, singing this song.

II

God for King Charles! Pym and such carles
To the Devil that prompts 'em their treasonous parles!
Cavaliers, up! Lips from the cup,
Hands from the pasty, nor bite take nor sup
Till you're—
CHORUS.—*Marching along, fifty score strong,*
Great-hearted gentlemen, singing this song.

III

Hampden to hell, and his obsequies knell.
Serve Hazelrig, Fiennes, and young Harry as well!
England, good cheer! Rupert is near!
Kentish and loyalists, keep we not here,
CHORUS.—*Marching along, fifty score strong,*
Great-hearted gentlemen, singing this song.

IV

Then, God for King Charles! Pym and his snarls
To the Devil that pricks on such pestilent carles!
Hold by the right, you double your might;
So, onward to Nottingham, fresh for the fight,
CHORUS.—*March we along, fifty score strong,*
Great-hearted gentlemen, singing this song!

II. GIVE A ROUSE

I

King Charles, and who'll do him right now?
King Charles, and who's ripe for fight now?
Give a rouse; here's, in hell's despite now,
King Charles!

II

Who gave me the goods that went since?
Who raised me the house that sank once?
Who helped me to gold I spent since?
Who found me in wine you drank once?
CHORUS.—*King Charles, and who'll do him right now?*
King Charles, and who's ripe for fight now?
Give a rouse; here's, in hell's despite now,
King Charles!

III

To whom used my boy George quaff else,
By the old fool's side that begot him?
For whom did he cheer and laugh else,
While Noll's damned troopers shot him?
CHORUS.—*King Charles, and who'll do him right now?*
King Charles, and who's ripe for fight now?
Give a rouse: here's, in hell's despite now,
King Charles!

III. BOOT AND SADDLE

I

Boot, saddle, to horse, and away!
Rescue my castle before the hot day
Brightens to blue from its silvery gray,
CHORUS.—*Boot, saddle, to horse, and away!*

II

Ride past the suburbs, asleep as you'd say;
Many's the friend there, will listen and pray
"God's luck to gallants that strike up the lay—
CHORUS.—"*Boot, saddle, to horse, and away*!"

III

Forty miles off, like a roebuck at bay,
Flouts castle Brancepeth the Roundheads' array:
Who laughs, "Good fellows ere this, by my fay,
CHORUS.—"*Boot, saddle, to horse, and away*!"

IV

Who? My wife Gertrude; that, honest and gay,

Laughs when you talk of surrendering, "Nay!

I've better counsellors; what counsel they?

CHORUS.—"*Boot, saddle, to horse, and away*!"

HOME-THOUGHTS, FROM THE SEA

Nobly, nobly, Cape Saint Vincent to the Northwest died away;
Sunset ran, one glorious blood-red, reeking into Cadiz Bay;
Bluish 'mid the burning water, full in face Trafalgar lay;
In the dimmest Northeast distance dawned Gibraltar grand and gray;
"Here and here did England help me: how can I help England?"—say,
Whoso turns as I, this evening, turn to God and pray,
While Jove's planet rises yonder, silent over Africa.

SUMMUM BONUM

All the breath and the bloom of the year in the bag of one bee:
All the wonder and wealth of the mine in the heart of one gem:
In the core of one pearl all the shade and the shine of the sea:
Breath and bloom, shade and shine,—wonder, wealth, and—how far above them—
Truth, that's brighter than gem,
Trust, that's purer than pearl,—
Brightest truth, purest trust in the universe,—all were for me
In the kiss of one girl.

A FACE

If one could have that little head of hers
    Painted upon a background of pure gold,
Such as the Tuscan's early art prefers!
    No shade encroaching on the matchless mould
Of those two lips, which should be opening soft
    In the pure profile; not as when she laughs,
For that spoils all: but rather as if aloft
    Yon hyacinth, she loves so, leaned its staff's
Burden of honey-colored buds to kiss
And capture 'twixt the lips apart for this.
Then her little neck, three fingers might surround,
How it should waver on the pale gold ground
Up to the fruit-shaped, perfect chin it lifts!
I know, Correggio loves to mass, in rifts
Of heaven, his angel faces, orb on orb
Breaking its outline, burning shades absorb:
But these are only massed there, I should think,
    Waiting to see some wonder momently
    Grow out, stand full, fade slow against the sky
    (That's the pale ground you'd see this sweet face by),
    All heaven, meanwhile, condensed into one eye
Which fears to lose the wonder, should it wink.

SONGS FROM 'PIPPA PASSES'

I

Day!
Faster and more fast,
O'er night's brim, day boils at last:
Boils, pure gold, o'er the cloud-cup's brim.
Where spurting and suppressed it lay,
For not a froth-flake touched the rim
Of yonder gap in the solid gray
Of the eastern cloud, an hour away;
But forth one wavelet, then another, curled,
Till the whole sunrise, not to be suppressed,
Rose, reddened, and its seething breast
Flickered in bounds, grew gold, then overflowed the world.

II

All service ranks the same with God:
If now, as formerly He trod
Paradise, His presence fills
Our earth, each only as God wills
Can work—God's puppets, best and worst,
Are we: there is no last nor first.

III

The year's at the spring
And day's at the morn:
Morning's at seven;
The hillside's dew-pearled;
The lark's on the wing;
The snail's on the thorn:
God's in His heaven—
All's right with the world!

IV

Give her but a least excuse to love me!
When—where—
How—can this arm establish her above me,
If fortune fixed her as my lady there,
There already, to eternally reprove me?
    ("Hist!"—said Kate the queen;
    But "Oh," cried the maiden, binding her tresses,
    "'Tis only a page that carols unseen,
    Crumbling your hounds their messes!")

Is she wronged?—To the rescue of her honour,
My heart!
Is she poor?—What costs it to be styled a donor?
Merely an earth to cleave, a sea to part.
But that fortune should have thrust all this upon her!

("Nay, list!"—bade Kate the queen;
And still cried the maiden, binding her tresses,
"'Tis only a page that carols unseen,
Fitting your hawks their jesses!")

THE LOST LEADER

I

Just for a handful of silver he left us,
    Just for a riband to stick in his coat—
Found the one gift of which fortune bereft us,
    Lost all the others she lets us devote;
They, with the gold to give, doled him out silver,
    So much was theirs who so little allowed;
How all our copper had gone for his service!
    Rags—were they purple, his heart had been proud!
We that had loved him so, followed him, honoured him,
    Lived in his mild and magnificent eye,
Learned his great language, caught his clear accents,
    Made him our pattern to live and to die!
Shakespeare was of us, Milton was for us,
    Burns, Shelley, were with us,—they watch from their graves!
He alone breaks from the van and the freemen,
    He alone sinks to the rear and the slaves!

II

We shall march prospering—not through his presence;
    Songs may inspirit us,—not from his lyre:
Deeds will be done,—while he boasts his quiescence,
    Still bidding crouch whom the rest bade aspire:

Blot out his name, then, record one lost soul more,
    One task more declined, one more footpath untrod,
One more devil's-triumph and sorrow for angels,
    One wrong more to man, one more insult to God!
Life's night begins: let him never come back to us!
    There would be doubt, hesitation, and pain,
Forced praise on our part—the glimmer of twilight,
    Never glad confident morning again!
Best fight on well, for we taught him—strike gallantly,
    Menace our heart ere we master his own;
Then let him receive the new knowledge and wait us,
    Pardoned in heaven, the first by the throne!

APPARENT FAILURE

"We shall soon lose a celebrated building."

—*Paris Newspaper.*

I

No, for I'll save it! Seven years since
    I passed through Paris, stopped a day
To see the baptism of your Prince,
    Saw, made my bow, and went my way:
Walking the heat and headache off,
    I took the Seine-side, you surmise,
Thought of the Congress, Gortschakoff,
    Cavour's appeal and Buol's replies,
So sauntered till—what met my eyes?

II

Only the Doric little Morgue!
    The dead-house where you show your drowned:
Petrarch's Vaucluse makes proud the Sorgue,
    Your Morgue has made the Seine renowned.
One pays one's debt in such a case;
    I plucked up heart and entered,—stalked,
Keeping a tolerable face
    Compared with some whose cheeks were chalked:
Let them! No Briton's to be balked!

III

First came the silent gazers; next,
    A screen of glass, we're thankful for;
Last, the sight's self, the sermon's text,
    The three men who did most abhor
Their life in Paris yesterday,
    So killed themselves: and now, enthroned
Each on his copper couch, they lay
    Fronting me, waiting to be owned.
I thought, and think, their sin's atoned.

IV

Poor men, God made, and all for that!
    The reverence struck me; o'er each head
Religiously was hung its hat,
    Each coat dripped by the owner's bed,
Sacred from touch: each had his berth,
    His bounds, his proper place of rest,
Who last night tenanted on earth
    Some arch, where twelve such slept abreast,—
Unless the plain asphalt seemed best.

V

How did it happen, my poor boy?
    You wanted to be Buonaparte
And have the Tuileries for toy,
    And could not, so it broke your heart?
You, old one by his side, I judge,
    Were, red as blood, a socialist,
A leveller! Does the Empire grudge
    You've gained what no Republic missed?
Be quiet, and unclench your fist!

VI

And this—why, he was red in vain,
    Or black,—poor fellow that is blue!
What fancy was it, turned your brain?
    Oh, women were the prize for you!
Money gets women, cards and dice
    Get money, and ill-luck gets just
The copper couch and one clear nice
    Cool squirt of water o'er your bust,
The right thing to extinguish lust!

VII

It's wiser being good than bad;
    It's safer being meek than fierce:
It's fitter being sane than mad.
    My own hope is, a sun will pierce
The thickest cloud earth ever stretched;
    That, after Last, returns the First,
Tho' a wide compass round be fetched;
    That what began best, can't end worst,
Nor what God blessed once, prove accurst.

FEARS AND SCRUPLES

I

Here's my case. Of old I used to love him.
    This same unseen friend, before I knew:
Dream there was none like him, none above him,—
    Wake to hope and trust my dream was true.

II

Loved I not his letters full of beauty?
    Not his actions famous far and wide?
Absent, he would know I vowed him duty,
    Present, he would find me at his side.

III

Pleasant fancy! for I had but letters,
    Only knew of actions by hearsay:
He himself was busied with my betters;
    What of that? My turn must come some day.

IV

"Some day" proving—no day! Here's the puzzle.
    Passed and passed my turn is. Why complain?
He's so busied! If I could but muzzle
    People's foolish mouths that give me pain!

V

"Letters?" (hear them!) "You a judge of writing?
  Ask the experts!—How they shake the head
O'er these characters, your friend's inditing—
  Call them forgery from A to Z!

VI

"Actions? Where's your certain proof" (they bother)
  "He, of all you find so great and good,
He, he only, claims this, that, the other
  Action—claimed by men, a multitude?"

VII

I can simply wish I might refute you,
  Wish my friend would,—by a word, a wink,—
Bid me stop that foolish mouth,—you brute you!
  He keeps absent,—why, I cannot think.

VIII

Never mind! Tho' foolishness may flout me.
  One thing's sure enough; 'tis neither frost,
No, nor fire, shall freeze or burn from out me
  Thanks for truth—tho' falsehood, gained—tho' lost.

IX

All my days, I'll go the softlier, sadlier,
    For that dream's sake! How forget the thrill
Thro' and thro' me as I thought, "The gladlier
    Lives my friend because I love him still!"

X

Ah, but there's a menace some one utters!
    "What and if your friend at home play tricks?
Peep at hide-and-seek behind the shutters?
    Mean your eyes should pierce thro' solid bricks?

XI

'What and if he, frowning, wake you, dreamy?
    Lay on you the blame that bricks—conceal?
Say '*At least I saw who did not see me,*
    Does see now, and presently shall feel'?"

XII

"Why, that makes your friend a monster!" say you;
    "Had his house no window? At first nod,
Would you not have hailed him?" Hush, I pray you!
    What if this friend happen to be—God?

INSTANS TYRANNUS

I

Of the million or two, more or less,
I rule and possess,
One man, for some cause undefined,
Was least to my mind.

II

I struck him, he grovelled of course—
For, what was his force?
I pinned him to earth with my weight
And persistence of hate;
And he lay, would not moan, would not curse,
As his lot might be worse.

III

"Were the object less mean, would he stand
At the swing of my hand!
For obscurity helps him, and blots
The hole where he squats."
So, I set my five wits on the stretch.
To inveigle the wretch.
All in vain! Gold and jewels I threw,
Still he couched there perdue;

I tempted his blood and his flesh,
Hid in roses my mesh,
Choicest cates and the flagon's best spilth:
Still he kept to his filth.

IV

Had he kith now or kin, were access
To his heart, did I press:
Just a son or a mother to seize!
No such booty as these.
Were it simply a friend to pursue
'Mid my million or two,
Who could pay me, in person or pelf,
What he owes me himself!
No: I could not but smile thro' my chafe:
For the fellow lay safe
As his mates do, the midge and the nit,
—Through minuteness, to wit.

V

Then a humour more great took its place
At the thought of his face:
The droop, the low cares of the mouth,
The trouble uncouth
'Twixt the brows, all that air one is fain
To put out of its pain,
And, "no!" I admonished myself,

"Is one mocked by an elf.
Is one baffled by toad or by rat?
The gravamen's in that!
How the lion, who crouches to suit
His back to my foot,
Would admire that I stand in debate!
But the small turns the great
If it vexes you,—that is the thing!
Toad or rat vex the king?
Tho' I waste half my realm to unearth
Toad or rat, 'tis well worth!"

VI

So, I soberly laid my last plan
To extinguish the man.
Round his creep-hole, with never a break
Ran my fires for his sake;
Overhead, did my thunder combine
With my under-ground mine:
Till I looked from my labour content
To enjoy the event.

VII

When sudden...how think ye, the end?
Did I say "without friend?"
Say rather, from marge to blue marge
The whole sky grew his targe

With the sun's self for visible boss,
While an Arm ran across
Which the earth heaved beneath like a breast!
Where the wretch was safe prest!
Do you see! Just my vengeance complete,
The man sprang to his feet,
Stood erect, caught at God's skirts, and prayed!
—So, *I* was afraid!

THE PATRIOT

AN OLD STORY

I

It was roses, roses, all the way,
    With myrtle mixed in my path like mad;
The house-roofs seemed to heave and sway,
    The church-spires flamed, such flags they had,
A year ago on this very day.

II

The air broke into a mist with bells,
    The old walls rocked with the crowd and cries.
Had I said, "Good folk, mere noise repels—
    But give me your sun from yonder skies!"
They had answered "And afterward, what else?"

III

Alack, it was I who leaped at the sun
    To give it my loving friends to keep!
Naught man could do, have I left undone:
    And you see my harvest, what I reap
This very day, now a year is run.

IV

There's nobody on the house-tops now—
    Just a palsied few at the windows set;
For the best of the sight is, all allow,
    At the Shambles' Gate—or, better yet,
By the very scaffold's foot, I trow.

V

I go in the rain, and, more than needs,
    A rope cuts both my wrists behind;
And I think, by the feel, my forehead bleeds,
    For they fling, whoever has a mind,
Stones at me for my year's misdeeds.

VI

Thus I entered, and thus I go!
    In triumphs, people have dropped down dead,
"Paid by the world, what dost thou owe
    Me?"—God might question; now instead,
'Tis God shall repay: I am safer so.

THE BOY AND THE ANGEL

Morning, evening, noon, and night,
"Praise God!" sang Theocrite.

Then to his poor trade he turned,
Whereby the daily meal was earned.

Hard he laboured, long and well;
O'er his work the boy's curls fell.

But ever, at each period,
He stopped and sang, "Praise God!"

Then back again his curls he threw,
And cheerful turned to work anew.

Said Blaise, the listening monk, "Well done;
I doubt not thou art heard, my son:

"As well as if thy voice to-day
Were praising God, the Pope's great way.

"This Easter Day, the Pope at Rome
Praises God from Peter's dome."

Said Theocrite, "Would God that I
Might praise Him that great way, and die!"

Night passed, day shone,
And Theocrite was gone.

With God a day endures alway,
A thousand years are but a day.

God said in heaven, "Nor day nor night
Now brings the voice of my delight."

Then Gabriel, like a rainbow's birth,
Spread his wings and sank to earth;

Entered, in flesh, the empty cell,
Lived there, and played the craftsman well;

And morning, evening, noon, and night,
Praised God in place of Theocrite.

And from a boy, to youth he grew:
The man put off the stripling's hue:

The man matured and fell away
Into the season of decay:

And ever o'er the trade he bent,
And ever lived on earth content.

(He did God's will; to him, all one
If on the earth or in the sun.)

God said, "A praise is in mine ear;
There is no doubt in it, no fear:

"So sing old worlds, and so
New worlds that from my footstool go.

"Clearer loves sound other ways:
I miss my little human praise."

Then forth sprang Gabriel's wings, off fell
The flesh disguise, remained the cell.

'Twas Easter day: he flew to Rome,
And paused above Saint Peter's dome.

In the tiring-room close by
The great outer gallery,

With his holy vestments dight,
Stood the new Pope, Theocrite:

And all his past career
Came back upon him clear,

Since when, a boy, he plied his trade,
Till on his life the sickness weighed;

And in his cell, when death drew near,
An angel in a dream brought cheer:

And rising from the sickness drear,
He grew a priest, and now stood here.

To the East with praise he turned,
And on his sight the angel burned.

"I bore thee from thy craftsman's cell,
And set thee here; I did not well.

"Vainly I left my angel-sphere,
Vain was thy dream of many a year,

"Thy voice's praise seemed weak; it dropped—
Creation's chorus stopped!

"Go back and praise again
The early way, while I remain.

"With that weak voice of our disdain,
Take up creation's pausing strain.

"Back to the cell and poor employ:
Resume the craftsman and the boy!"

Theocrite grew old at home;
A new Pope dwelt in Peter's dome.

One vanished as the other died:
They sought God side by side.

MEMORABILIA

I

Ah, did you once see Shelley plain,
And did he stop and speak to you,
And did you speak to him again?
How strange it seems and new!

II

But you were living before that,
And also you are living after;
And the memory I started at—
My starting moves your laughter!

III

I crossed a moor with a name of its own
And a certain use in the world, no doubt,
Yet a hand's-breadth of it shines alone
'Mid the blank miles round about.

IV

For there I picked upon the heather
And there I put inside my breast
A moulted feather, an eagle-feather!
Well, I forget the rest.

WHY I AM A LIBERAL

"Why?" Because all I haply can and do,
All that I am now, all I hope to be,—
Whence comes it save from fortune setting free
Body and soul the purpose to pursue,
God traced for both? If fetters, not a few,
Of prejudice, convention, fall from me,
These shall I bid men—each in his degree
Also God-guided—bear, and gayly too?
But little do or can the best of us:
That little is achieved thro' Liberty.
Who then dares hold, emancipated thus,
His fellow shall continue bound? not I,
Who live, love, labour freely, nor discuss
A brother's right to freedom. That is "Why."

PROSPICE

Fear death? to feel the fog in my throat,
The mist in my face,
When the snows begin, and the blasts denote
I am nearing the place,
The power of the night, the press of the storm,
The post of the foe;
Where he stands, the Arch Fear in a visible form,
Yet the strong man must go:
For the journey is done and the summit attained,
And the barriers fall,
Though a battle's to fight ere the guerdon be gained,
The reward of it all.
I was ever a fighter, so—one fight more,
The best and the last!
I would hate that death bandaged my eyes, and forbore,
And bade me creep past,
No! let me taste the whole of it, fare like my peers
The heroes of old,
Bear the brunt, in a minute pay glad life's arrears
Of pain, darkness, and cold.
For sudden the worst turns the best to the brave,
The black minute's at end,
And the elements' rage, the fiend-voices that rave,
Shall dwindle, shall blend,

Shall change, shall become first a peace out of pain,
    Then a light, then thy breast,
O thou soul of my soul! I shall clasp thee again,
    And with God be the rest!

EPILOGUE TO "ASOLANDO"

At the midnight in the silence of the sleep-time,
When you set your fancies free,
Will they pass to where—by death, fools think, imprisoned—
Low he lies who once so loved you whom you loved so,
—Pity me?

Oh to love so, be so loved, yet so mistaken!
What had I on earth to do
With the slothful, with the mawkish, the unmanly?
Like the aimless, helpless, hopeless, did I drivel
—Being—who?

One who never turned his back but marched breast forward,
Never doubted clouds would break,
Never dreamed, tho' right were worsted, wrong would triumph,
Held we fall to rise, are baffled to fight better,
Sleep to wake.

No, at noonday in the bustle of man's work-time
Greet the unseen with a cheer!
Bid him forward, breast and back as either should be,
"Strive and thrive!" cry "Speed,—fight on, fare ever
There as here!"

"DE GUSTIBUS—"

I

Your ghost will walk, you lover of trees,
    (If our loves remain)
    In an English lane,
By a cornfield-side a-flutter with poppies.
Hark, those two in the hazel coppice—
A boy and a girl, if the good fates please,
    Making love, say,—
    The happier they!
Draw yourself up from the light of the moon.
And let them pass, as they will too soon,
    With the beanflower's boon,
    And the blackbird's tune,
    And May, and June!

II

What I love best in all the world
Is a castle, precipice-encurled,
In a gash of the wind-grieved Apennine.
Or look for me, old fellow of mine,
(If I get my head from out the mouth
O'the grave, and loose my spirit's bands,
And come again to the land of lands)—
In a sea-side house to the farther South,

Where the baked cicala dies of drouth,
And one sharp tree—'tis a cypress—stands,
By the many hundred years red-rusted,
Bough iron-spiked, ripe fruit-o'ercrusted,
My sentinel to guard the sands
To the water's edge. For, what expands
Before the house, but the great opaque
Blue breadth of sea without a break?
While, in the house, forever crumbles
Some fragment of the frescoed walls,
From blisters where a scorpion sprawls.
A girl bare-footed brings, and tumbles
Down on the pavement, green-flesh melons,
And says there's news to-day—the king
Was shot at, touched in the liver-wing,
Goes with his Bourbon arm in a sling:
—She hopes they have not caught the felons.
Italy, my Italy!
Queen Mary's saying serves for me—
        (When fortune's malice
        Lost her, Calais)
Open my heart and you will see
Graved inside of it, "Italy."
Such lovers old are I and she:
So it always was, so shall ever be!

THE ITALIAN IN ENGLAND

That second time they hunted me
From hill to plain, from shore to sea,
And Austria, hounding far and wide
Her blood-hounds thro' the country-side,
Breathed hot an instant on my trace,—
I made, six days, a hiding-place
Of that dry green old aqueduct
Where I and Charles, when boys, have plucked
The fire-flies from the roof above,
Bright creeping thro' the moss they love:
—How long it seems since Charles was lost!
Six days the soldiers crossed, and crossed
The country in my very sight;
And when that peril ceased at night,
The sky broke out in red dismay
With signal-fires. Well, there I lay
Close covered o'er in my recess,
Up to the neck in ferns and cress.
Thinking on Metternich, our friend,
And Charles's miserable end,
And much beside, two days; the third,
Hunger o'ercame me when I heard
The peasants from the village go
To work among the maize: you know,
With us in Lombardy, they bring
Provisions packed on mules, a string,

With little bells that cheer their task,
And casks, and boughs on every cask
To keep the sun's heat from the wine;
These I let pass in jingling line;
And, close on them, dear noisy crew,
The peasants from the village, too;
For at the very rear would troop
Their wives and sisters in a group
To help, I knew. When these had passed,
I threw my glove to strike the last,
Taking the chance: she did not start,
Much less cry out, but stooped apart,
One instant rapidly glanced round,
And saw me beckon from the ground.
A wild bush grows and hides my crypt;
She picked my glove up while she stripped
A branch off, then rejoined the rest
With that; my glove lay in her breast:
Then I drew breath; they disappeared:
It was for Italy I feared.

An hour, and she returned alone
Exactly where my glove was thrown.
Meanwhile came many thoughts: on me
Rested the hopes of Italy.
I had devised a certain tale
Which, when 'twas told her, could not fail
Persuade a peasant of its truth;
I meant to call a freak of youth

This hiding, and give hopes of pay,
And no temptation to betray.
But when I saw that woman's face,
Its calm simplicity of grace,
Our Italy's own attitude
In which she walked thus far, and stood,
Planting each naked foot so firm,
To crush the snake and spare the worm—
At first sight of her eyes, I said,
"I am that man upon whose head
They fix the price, because I hate
The Austrians over us; the State
Will give you gold—oh, gold so much!—
If you betray me to their clutch.
And be your death, for aught I know,
If once they find you saved their foe.
Now, you must bring me food and drink,
And also paper, pen and ink,
And carry safe what I shall write
To Padua, which you'll reach at night
Before the duomo shuts; go in,
And wait till Tenebrae begin;
Walk to the third confessional,
Between the pillar and the wall,
And kneeling whisper, *Whence comes peace?*
Say it a second time, then cease;
And if the voice inside returns,
From Christ and Freedom; what concerns
The cause of Peace?—for answer, slip

My letter where you placed your lip;
Then come back happy we have done
Our mother service—I, the son,
As you the daughter of our land!"

Three mornings more, she took her stand
In the same place, with the same eyes:
I was no surer of sun-rise
Than of her coming. We conferred
Of her own prospects, and I heard
She had a lover—stout and tall,
She said—then let her eyelids fall,
"He could do much"—as if some doubt
Entered her heart,—then, passing out,
"She could not speak for others, who
Had other thoughts; herself she knew;"
And so she brought me drink and food.
After four days, the scouts pursued
Another path; at last arrived
The help my Paduan friends contrived
To furnish me: she brought the news.
For the first time I could not choose
But kiss her hand, and lay my own
Upon her head—"This faith was shown
To Italy, our mother; she
Uses my hand and blesses thee."
She followed down to the sea-shore;
I left and never saw her more.

How very long since I have thought
Concerning—much less wished for—aught
Beside the good of Italy,
For which I live and mean to die!
I never was in love; and since
Charles proved false, what shall now convince
My inmost heart I have a friend?
However, if I pleased to spend
Real wishes on myself—say, three—
I know at least what one should be.
I would grasp Metternich until
I felt his red wet throat distil
In blood thro' these two hands. And next,
—Nor much for that am I perplexed—
Charles, perjured traitor, for his part,
Should die slow of a broken heart
Under his new employers. Last
—Ah, there, what should I wish? For fast
Do I grow old and out of strength.
If I resolved to seek at length
My father's house again, how scared
They all would look, and unprepared!
My brothers live in Austria's pay
—Disowned me long ago, men say;
And all my early mates who used
To praise me so—perhaps induced
More than one early step of mine—
Are turning wise: while some opine
"Freedom grows license," some suspect

"Haste breeds delay," and recollect
They always said, such premature
Beginnings never could endure!
So, with a sullen "All's for best,"
The land seems settling to its rest.
I think then, I should wish to stand
This evening in that dear, lost land,
Over the sea the thousand miles,
And know if yet that woman smiles
With the calm smile; some little farm
She lives in there, no doubt: what harm
If I sat on the door-side bench,
And while her spindle made a trench
Fantastically in the dust,
Inquired of all her fortunes—just
Her children's ages and their names,
And what may be the husband's aims
For each of them. I'd talk this out,
And sit there, for an hour about,
Then kiss her hand once more, and lay
Mine on her head, and go my way.

So much for idle wishing—how
It steals the time! To business now.

MY LAST DUCHESS

FERRARA

That's my last Duchess painted on the wall,
Looking as if she were alive. I call
That piece a wonder, now: Frà Pandolf's hands
Worked busily a day, and there she stands.
Will't please you sit and look at her? I said
"Frà Pandolf" by design: for never read
Strangers like you that pictured countenance,
The depth and passion of its earnest glance,
But to myself they turned (since none puts by
The curtain I have drawn for you, but I)
And seemed as they would ask me, if they durst,
How such a glance came there; so, not the first
Are you to turn and ask thus. Sir, 'twas not
Her husband's presence only, called that spot
Of joy into the Duchess' cheek: perhaps
Frà Pandolf chanced to say "Her mantle laps
Over my lady's wrist too much," or "Paint
Must never hope to reproduce the faint
Half-flush that dies along her throat:" such stuff
Was courtesy, she thought, and cause enough
For calling up that spot of joy. She had
A heart—how shall I say?—too soon made glad,
Too easily impressed; she liked whate'er
She looked on, and her looks went everywhere.

Sir, 'twas all one! My favour at her breast,
The dropping of the daylight in the West,
The bough of cherries some officious fool
Broke in the orchard for her, the white mule
She rode with round the terrace—all and each
Would draw from her alike the approving speech,
Or blush, at least. She thanked men,—good! but thanked
Somehow—I know not how—as if she ranked
My gift of a nine-hundred-years-old name
With anybody's gift. Who'd stoop to blame
This sort of trifling? Even had you skill
In speech—(which I have not)—to make your will
Quite clear to such an one, and say, "Just this
Or that in you disgusts me; here you miss,
Or there exceed the mark"—and if she let
Herself be lessoned so, nor plainly set
Her wits to yours, forsooth, and made excuse,
—E'en then would be some stooping: and I choose
Never to stoop. Oh, sir, she smiled, no doubt,
Whene'er I passed her; but who passed without
Much the same smile? This grew; I gave commands;
Then all smiles stopped together. There she stands
As if alive. Will't please you rise? We'll meet
The company below, then. I repeat,
The Count your master's known munificence
Is ample warrant that no just pretence
Of mine for dowry will be disallowed;
Though his fair daughter's self, as I avowed

At starting, is my object. Nay, we'll go
Together down, sir. Notice Neptune, though,
Taming a sea-horse, thought a rarity,
Which Claus of Innsbruck cast in bronze for me!

THE BISHOP ORDERS HIS TOMB AT SAINT PRAXED'S CHURCH

ROME, 15—

Vanity, saith the preacher, vanity!
Draw round my bed: is Anselm keeping back?
Nephews—sons mine...ah God, I know not! Well,
She, men would have to be your mother once,
Old Gandolf envied me, so fair she was!
What's done is done, and she is dead beside,
Dead long ago, and I am Bishop since.
And as she died so must we die ourselves,
And thence ye may perceive the world's a dream.
Life, how and what is it? As here I lie
In this state-chamber, dying by degrees,
Hours and long hours in the dead night, I ask
"Do I live, am I dead?" Peace, peace seems all.
Saint Praxed's ever was the church for peace;
And so, about this tomb of mine. I fought
With tooth and nail to save my niche, ye know:
—Old Gandolf cozened me, despite my care;
Shrewd was that snatch from out the corner South
He graced his carrion with, God curse the same!
Yet still my niche is not so cramped but thence
One sees the pulpit o' the epistle-side,
And somewhat of the choir, those silent seats,
And up into the aery dome where live

The angels, and a sunbeam's sure to lurk:
And I shall fill my slab of basalt there,
And 'neath my tabernacle take my rest,
With those nine columns round me, two and two,
The odd one at my feet where Anselm stands:
Peach-blossom marble all, the rare, the ripe
As fresh-poured red wine of a mighty pulse,
—Old Gandolf with his paltry onion-stone,
Put me where I may look at him! True peach,
Rosy and flawless: how I earned the prize!
Draw close: that conflagration of my church
—What then? So much was saved if aught were missed!
My sons, ye would not be my death? Go dig
The white-grape vineyard where the oil-press stood,
Drop water gently till the surface sink,
And if ye find...Ah God, I know not, I!...
Bedded in store of rotten fig-leaves soft,
And corded up in a tight olive-frail,
Some lump, ah God, of *lapis lazuli*,
Big as a Jew's head cut off at the nape,
Blue as a vein o'er the Madonna's breast...
Sons, all have I bequeathed you, villas, all,
That brave Frascati villa, with its bath,
So, let the blue lump poise between my knees,
Like God the Father's globe on both his hands
Ye worship in the Jesu Church, so gay,
For Gandolf shall not choose but see and burst!
Swift as a weaver's shuttle fleet our years:
Man goeth to the grave, and where is he?

Did I say, basalt for my slab, sons? Black—
'Twas ever antique-black I meant! How else
Shall ye contrast my frieze to come beneath?
The bas-relief in bronze ye promised me,
Those Pans and Nymphs ye wot of, and perchance
Some tripod, thyrsus, with a vase or so,
The Saviour at his sermon on the mount,
Saint Praxed in a glory, and one Pan
Ready to twitch the Nymph's last garment off,
And Moses with the tables...but I know
Ye mark me not! What do they whisper thee,
Child of my bowels, Anselm? Ah, ye hope
To revel down my villas while I gasp
Bricked o'er with beggar's mouldy travertine
Which Gandolf from his tomb-top chuckles at!
Nay, boys, ye love me—all of jasper, then!
'Tis jasper ye stand pledged to, lest I grieve
My bath must needs be left behind, alas!
One block, pure green as a pistachio-nut,
There's plenty jasper somewhere in the world—
And have I not Saint Praxed's ear to pray
Horses for ye, and brown Greek manuscripts,
And mistresses with great smooth marbly limbs?
—That's if ye carve my epitaph aright,
Choice Latin, picked phrase, Tully's every word,
No gaudy ware like Gandolf's second line—
Tully, my masters? Ulpian serves his need!
And then how I shall lie thro' centuries,
And hear the blessed mutter of the mass,

And see God made and eaten all day long,
And feel the steady candle-flame, and taste
Good strong thick stupefying incense-smoke!
For as I lie here, hours of the dead night,
Dying in state and by such slow degrees,
I fold my arms as if they clasped a crook,
And stretch my feet forth straight as stone can point,
And let the bedclothes, for a mortcloth, drop
Into great laps and folds of sculptor's-work:
And as yon tapers dwindle, and strange thoughts
Grow, with a certain humming in my ears,
About the life before I lived this life,
And this life too, popes, cardinals, and priests,
Saint Praxed at his sermon on the mount,
Your tall pale mother with her talking eyes,
And new-found agate urns as fresh as day,
And marble's language, Latin pure, discreet,
—Aha, ELUCESCEBAT quoth our friend?
No Tully, said I, Ulpian at the best!
Evil and brief hath been my pilgrimage.
All *lapis*, all, sons! Else I give the Pope
My villas! Will ye ever eat my heart?
Ever your eyes were as a lizard's quick,
They glitter like your mother's for my soul.
Or ye would heighten my impoverished frieze,
Piece out its starved design, and fill my vase
With grapes, and add a visor and a Term,
And to the tripod ye would tie a lynx
That in his struggle throws the thyrsus down,

To comfort me on my entablature
Whereon I am to lie till I must ask
"Do I live, am I dead?" There, leave me, there!
For ye have stabbed me with ingratitude
To death—ye wish it—God, ye wish it! stone—
Gritstone, a-crumble! clammy squares which sweat
As if the corpse they keep were oozing through—
And no more *lapis* to delight the world!
Well, go! I bless ye. Fewer tapers there,
But in a row: and, going, turn your backs
—Ay, like departing altar-ministrants,
And leave me in my church, the church for peace,
That I may watch, at leisure if he leers—
Old Gandolf—at me, from his onion-stone,
As still he envied me, so fair she was!

THE LABORATORY

ANCIEN REGIME

I

Now that I, tying thy glass mask tightly,
May gaze through these faint smokes curling whitely,
As thou pliest thy trade in this devil's-smithy—
Which is the poison to poison her, prithee?

II

He is with her, and they know that I know
Where they are, what they do: they believe my tears flow
While they laugh, laugh at me, at me fled to the drear
Empty church, to pray God in, for them!—I am here!

III

Grind away, moisten and mash up thy paste,
Pound at thy powder, I am not in haste!
Better sit thus and observe thy strange things,
Than go where men wait me, and dance at the King's.

IV

That in the mortar—you call it a gum?
Ah, the brave tree whence such gold oozings come!
And yonder soft phial, the exquisite blue,
Sure to taste sweetly,—is that poison, too?

V

Had I but all of them, thee and thy treasures,
What a wild crowd of Invisible pleasures!
To carry pure death in an earring, a casket,
A signet, a fan-mount, a filigree basket!

VI

Soon, at the King's, a mere lozenge to give
And Pauline should have just thirty minutes to live!
But to light a pastille, and Elise, with her head
And her breast and her arms and her hands, should drop dead!

VII

Quick—is it finished? The colour's too grim!
Why not soft like the phial's, enticing and dim?
Let it brighten her drink, let her turn it and stir,
And try it and taste, ere she fix and prefer!

VIII

What a drop! She's not little, no minion like me!
That's why she ensnared him: this never will free
The soul from those masculine eyes,—say "No!"
To that pulse's magnificent come-and-go.

IX

For only last night, as they whispered, I brought
My own eyes to bear on her so that I thought
Could I keep them one half-minute fixed, she would fall
Shrivelled; she fell not: yet this does it all!

X

Not that I bid you spare her the pain;
Let death be felt and the proof remain:
Brand, burn up, bite into its grace—
He is sure to remember her dying face!

XI

Is it done? Take my mask off! Nay, be not morose;
It kills her, and this prevents seeing it close:
The delicate droplet, my whole fortune's fee!
If it hurts her, beside, can it ever hurt me?

XII

Now, take all my jewels, gorge gold to your fill,
You may kiss me, old man, on my mouth if you will!
But brush this dust off me, lest horror it brings
Ere I know it—next moment I dance at the King's!

HOME THOUGHTS, FROM ABROAD

I

Oh, to be in England
Now that April's there,
And whoever wakes in England
Sees, some morning, unaware,
That the lowest boughs and the brushwood sheaf
Round the elm-tree bole are in tiny leaf,
While the chaffinch sings on the orchard bough
In England—now!

II

And after April, when May follows,
And the white-throat builds, and all the swallows!
Hark I where my blossomed pear tree in the hedge
Leans to the field and scatters on the clover
Blossoms and dewdrops—at the bent spray's edge—
That's the wise thrush; he sings each song twice over,
Lest you should think he never could recapture
The first fine careless rapture!
And though the fields look rough with hoary dew,
All will be gay when noontide wakes anew
The buttercups, the little children's dower
—Far brighter than this gaudy melon-flower!

UP AT A VILLA—DOWN IN THE CITY

(As distinguished by an Italian person of quality.)

I

Had I but plenty of money, money enough and to spare,
The house for me, no doubt, were a house in the city square;
Ah, such a life, such a life, as one leads at the window there!

II

Something to see, by Bacchus, something to hear, at least!
There, the whole day long, one's life is a perfect feast;
While up at a villa one lives, I maintain it, no more than a beast.

III

Well now, look at our villa! stuck like the horn of a bull
Just on a mountain edge as bare as the creature's skull,
Save a mere shag of a bush with hardly a leaf to pull!
—I scratch my own, sometimes, to see if the hair's turned wool.

IV

But the city, oh the city—the square with the houses! Why?
They are stone-faced, white as a curd, there's something to take the eye!
Houses in four straight lines, not a single front awry;
You watch who crosses and gossips, who saunters, who hurries by;
Green blinds, as a matter of course, to draw when the sun gets high;
And the shops with fanciful signs which are painted properly.

V

What of a villa? Tho' winter be over in March, by rights,
'Tis May perhaps ere the snow shall have withered well off the heights:
You've the brown ploughed land before, where the oxen steam and wheeze,
And the hills over-smoked behind by the faint gray olive trees.

VI

Is it better in May, I ask you? You've summer all at once;
In a day he leaps complete with a few strong April suns,
'Mid the sharp short emerald wheat, scarce risen three fingers well,
The wild tulip, at end of its tube, blows out its great red bell
Like a thin clear bubble of blood, for the children to pick and sell.

VII

Is it ever hot in the square? There's a fountain to spout and splash!
In the shade it sings and springs; in the shine such foam-bows flash
On the horses with curling fish-tails, that prance and paddle and pash
Round the lady atop in her conch—fifty gazers do not abash,
Tho' all that she wears is some weeds round her waist in a sort of sash.

VIII

All the year long at the villa, nothing to see though you linger,
Except yon cypress that points like death's lean lifted forefinger.
Some think fireflies pretty, when they mix i' the corn and mingle,
Or thrid the stinking hemp till the stalks of it seem a-tingle.
Late August or early September, the stunning cicala is shrill,
And the bees keep their tiresome whine round the resinous firs on the hill.
Enough of the seasons,—I spare you the months of the fever and chill.

IX

Ere you open your eyes in the city, the blessed church-bells begin:
No sooner the bells leave off than the diligence rattles in:
You get the pick of the news, and it costs you never a pin.
By and by there's the travelling doctor gives pills, lets blood, draws teeth;
Or the Pulcinello-trumpet breaks up the market beneath.
At the post-office such a scene-picture—the new play, piping hot!
And a notice how, only this morning, three liberal thieves were shot.
Above it, behold the Archbishop's most fatherly of rebukes,
And beneath, with his crown and his lion, some little new law of the Duke's!

Or a sonnet with flowery marge, to the Reverend Don So-and-so,

Who is Dante, Boccaccio, Petrarca, St. Jerome and Cicero,

"And moreover" (the sonnet goes rhyming), "the skirts of St. Paul has reached,

Having preached us those six Lent-lectures more unctuous than ever he preached."

Noon strikes,—here sweeps the procession! our Lady borne smiling and smart.

With a pink gauze gown all spangles, and seven swords stuck in her heart!

Bang-whang-whang goes the drum, *tootle-te-tootle* the fife;

No keeping one's haunches still: it's the greatest pleasure in life.

X

But bless you, it's dear—it's dear! fowls, wine, at double the rate.

They have clapped a new tax upon salt, and what oil pays passing the gate

It's a horror to think of. And so, the villa for me, not the city!

Beggars can scarcely be choosers: but still—ah, the pity, the pity!

Look, two and two go the priests, then the monks with cowls and sandals,

And the penitents dressed in white shirts, a-holding the yellow candles;

One, he carries a flag up straight, and another a cross with handles,

And the Duke's guard brings up the rear, for the better prevention of scandals:

Bang-whang-whang goes the drum, *tootle-te-tootle* the fife.

Oh, a day in the city square, there is no such pleasure in life!

A TOCCATA OF GALUPPI'S

I

Oh Galuppi Baldassaro, this is very sad to find!
I can hardly misconceive you; it would prove me deaf and blind;
But altho' I take your meaning, 'tis with such a heavy mind!

II

Here you come with your old music, and here's all the good it brings.
What, they lived once thus at Venice where the merchants were the kings,
Where St. Mark's is, where the Doges used to wed the sea with rings?

III

Ay, because the sea's the street there; and 'tis arched by...what you call
...Shylock's bridge with houses on it, where they kept the carnival:
I was never out of England—it's as if I saw it all.

IV

Did young people take their pleasure when the sea was warm in May?
Balls and masks begun at midnight, burning ever to mid-day,
When they make up fresh adventures for the morrow, do you say?

V

Was a lady such a lady, cheeks so round and lips so red,—
On her neck the small face buoyant, like a bell-flower on its bed,
O'er the breast's superb abundance where a man might base his head?

VI

Well, and it was graceful of them: they'd break talk off and afford
—She, to bite her mask's black velvet—he, to finger on his sword,
While you sat and played Toccatas, stately at the clavichord?

VII

What? Those lesser thirds so plaintive, sixths diminished sigh on sigh,
Told them something? Those suspensions, those solutions—"Must we die?"
Those commiserating sevenths—"Life might last! we can but try!"

VIII

"Were you happy?"—"Yes."—"And are you still as happy?"—"Yes. And you?"
—"Then, more kisses!"—"Did *I* stop them, when, a million seemed so few?"
Hark, the dominant's persistence till it must be answered to!

IX

So, an octave struck the answer. Oh, they praised you, I dare say!
"Brave Galuppi! that was music! good alike at grave and gay!
I can always leave off talking when I hear a master play!"

X

Then they left you for their pleasure: till in due time, one by one,
Some with lives that came to nothing, some with deeds as well undone,
Death, stepped tacitly and took them where they never see the sun.

XI

But when I sit down to reason, think to take my stand nor swerve,
While I triumph o'er a secret wrung from nature's close reserve,
In you come with your cold music till I creep thro' every nerve.

XII

Yes, you, like a ghostly cricket, creaking where a house was burned:
"Dust and ashes, dead and done with, Venice spent what Venice earned.
The soul, doubtless, is immortal—where a soul can be discerned.

XIII

"Yours, for instance: you know physics, something of geology,
Mathematics are your pastime; souls shall rise in their degree;
Butterflies may dread extinction,—you'll not die, it cannot be!

XIV

"As for Venice and her people, merely born to bloom and drop,
Here on earth they bore their fruitage, mirth and folly were the crop:
What of soul was left, I wonder, when the kissing had to stop?

XV

"Dust and ashes!" So you creak it, and I want the heart to scold.
Dear dead women, with such hair, too—what's become of all the gold
Used to hang and brush their bosoms? I feel chilly and grown old.

ABT VOGLER

(AFTER HE HAS BEEN EXTEMPORIZING UPON THEMUSICAL INSTRUMENT OF HIS INVENTION)

I

Would that the structure brave, the manifold music I build,
Bidding my organ obey, calling its keys to their work,
Claiming each slave of the sound, at a touch, as when Solomon willed
Armies of angels that soar, legions of demons that lurk,
Man, brute, reptile, fly,—alien of end and of aim,
Adverse, each from the other heaven-high, hell-deep removed,—
Should rush into sight at once as he named the ineffable Name,
And pile him a palace straight, to pleasure the princess he loved!

II

Would it might tarry like his, the beautiful building of mine,
This which my keys in a crowd pressed and importuned to raise!
Ah, one and all, how they helped, would dispart now and now combine,
Zealous to hasten the work, heighten their master his praise!
And one would bury his brow with a blind plunge down to hell,
Burrow awhile and build, broad on the roots of things,
Then up again swim into sight, having based me my palace well,
Founded it, fearless of flame, flat on the nether springs.

III

And another would mount and march, like the excellent minion he was,
    Ay, another and yet another, one crowd but with many a crest,
Raising my rampired walls of gold as transparent as glass,
    Eager to do and die, yield each his place to the rest:
For higher still and higher (as a runner tips with fire,
    When a great illumination surprises a festal night—
Outlining round and round Rome's dome from space to spire)
    Up, the pinnacled glory reached, and the pride of my soul was in sight.

IV

In sight? Not half! for it seemed, it was certain, to match man's birth,
    Nature in turn conceived, obeying an impulse as I;
And the emulous heaven yearned down, made effort to reach the earth.
    As the earth had done her best, in my passion, to scale the sky:
Novel splendours burst forth, grew familiar and dwelt with mine.
    Not a point nor peak but found and fixed its wandering star;
Meteor-moons, balls of blaze: and they did not pale nor pine,
    For earth had attained to heaven, there was no more near nor far.

V

Nay more; for there wanted not who walked, in the glare and glow,
    Presences plain in the place; or, fresh, from the Protoplast,
Furnished for ages to come, when a kindlier wind should blow,
    Lured now to begin and live, in a house to their liking at last:

Or else the wonderful Dead who have passed thro' the body and gone,
    But were back once more to breathe in an old world worth their new:
What never had been, was now; what was, as it shall be anon;
    And what is,—shall I say, matched both? for I was made perfect too.

VI

All thro' my keys that gave their sounds to a wish of my soul,
    All thro' my soul that praised as its wish flowed visibly forth,
All thro' music and me! For think, had I painted the whole,
    Why, there it had stood, to see, nor the process so wonder-worth:
Had I written the same, made verse—still, effect proceeds from cause,
    Ye know why the forms are fair, ye hear how the tale is told;
It is all triumphant art, but art in obedience to laws,
    Painter and poet are proud, in the artist-list enrolled:—

VII

But here is the finger of God, a flash of the will that can,
    Existent behind all laws, that made them, and, lo, they are!
And I know not if, save in this, such gift be allowed to man,
    That out of three sounds he frame, not a fourth sound, but a star.
Consider it well: each tone of our scale in itself is naught;
    It is everywhere in the world—loud, soft, and all is said:
Give it to me to use! I mix it with two in my thought,
    And, there! Ye have heard and seen; consider and bow the head!

VIII

Well, it is gone at last, the palace of music I reared;
    Gone! and the good tears start, the praises that come too slow;
For one is assured at first, one scarce can say that he feared,
    That he even gave it a thought, the gone thing was to go.
Never to be again! But many more of the kind
    As good, nay, better perchance: is this your comfort to me?
To me, who must be saved because I cling with my mind
    To the same, same self, same love, same God: ay, what was, shall be.

IX

Therefore to whom turn I but to Thee, the ineffable Name?
    Builder and maker, Thou, of houses not made with hands!
What, have fear of change from Thee who art ever the same?
    Doubt that Thy power can fill the heart that Thy power expands?
There shall never be one lost good! What was, shall live as before;
    The evil is null, is naught, is silence implying sound;
What was good, shall be good, with, for evil, so much good more;
    On the earth the broken arcs; in the heaven, a perfect round.

X

All we have willed or hoped or dreamed of good shall exist;
    Not its semblance, but itself; no beauty, nor good, nor power
Whose voice has gone forth, but each survives for the melodist,
    When eternity affirms the conception of an hour.

The high that proved too high, the heroic for earth too hard.
  The passion that left the ground to lose itself in the sky,
Are music sent up to God by the lover and the bard;
  Enough that he heard it once; we shall hear it by and by.

XI

And what is our failure here but a triumph's evidence
  For the fulness of the days? Have we withered or agonized?
Why else was the pause prolonged but that singing might issue thence?
  Why rushed the discords in but that harmony should be prized?
Sorrow is hard to bear, and doubt is slow to clear,
  Each sufferer says his say, his scheme of the weal and woe:
But God has a few of us whom He whispers in the ear;
  The rest may reason and welcome; 'tis we musicians know.

XII

Well, it is earth with me; silence resumes her reign:
  I will be patient and proud, and soberly acquiesce.
Give me the keys. I feel for the common chord again,
  Sliding by semitones, till I sink to the minor,—yes,
And I blunt it into a ninth, and I stand on alien ground,
  Surveying awhile the heights I rolled from into the deep:
Which, hark, I have dared and done, for my resting-place is found,
  The C Major of this life: so, now I will try to sleep.

RABBI BEN EZRA

I

Grow old along with me!
The best is yet to be,
The last of life, for which the first was made:
Our times are in His hand
Who saith "A whole I planned,
Youth shows but half; trust God: see all, nor be afraid!"

II

Not that, amassing flowers,
Youth sighed, "Which rose make ours,
Which lily leave and then as best recall!"
Not that, admiring stars,
It yearned "Nor Jove, nor Mars;
Mine be some figured flame which blends, transcends them all!"

III

Not for such hopes and fears
Annulling youth's brief years,
Do I remonstrate: folly wide the mark!
Rather I prize the doubt
Low kinds exist without,
Finished and finite clods, untroubled by a spark.

IV

Poor vaunt of life indeed,
Were man but formed to feed
On joy, to solely seek and find and feast:
Such feasting ended, then
As sure an end to men;
Irks care the crop-full bird? Frets doubt the maw-crammed beast?

V

Rejoice we are allied
To That which doth provide
And not partake, effect and not receive!
A spark disturbs our clod;
Nearer we hold of God.
Who gives, than of His tribes that take, I must believe.

VI

Then, welcome each rebuff
That turns earth's smoothness rough,
Each sting that bids nor sit nor stand but go!
Be our joys three-parts pain!
Strive, and hold cheap the strain;
Learn, nor account the pang; dare, never grudge the throe!

VII

For thence,—a paradox
Which comforts while it mocks,—
Shall life succeed in that it seems to fail:
What I aspired to be,
And was not, comforts me:
A brute I might have been, but would not sink i'the scale.

VIII

What is he but a brute
Whose flesh has soul to suit,
Whose spirit works lest arms and legs want play?
To man, propose this test—
Thy body at its best,
How far can that project thy soul on its lone way?

IX

Yet gifts should prove their use:
I own the Past profuse
Of power each side, perfection every turn:
Eyes, ears took in their dole,
Brain treasured up the whole;
Should not the heart beat once "How good to live and learn?"

X

Not once beat "Praise be Thine!
I see the whole design,
I, who saw power, see now love perfect too:
Perfect I call Thy plan:
Thanks that I was a man!
Maker, remake, complete,—I trust what Thou shall do!"

XI

For pleasant is this flesh;
Our soul, in its rose-mesh
Pulled ever to the earth, still yearns for rest:
Would we some prize might hold
To match those manifold
Possessions of the brute,—gain most, as we did best!

XII

Let us not always say,
"Spite of this flesh to-day
I strove, made head, gained ground upon the whole!"
As the bird wings and sings,
Let us cry "All good things
Are ours, nor soul helps flesh more, now, than flesh helps soul!"

XIII

Therefore I summon age
To grant youth's heritage,
Life's struggle having so far reached its term:
Thence shall I pass, approved
A man, for aye removed
From the developed brute; a God tho' in the germ.

XIV

And I shall thereupon
Take rest, ere I be gone
Once more on my adventure brave and new:
Fearless and unperplexed,
When I wage battle next,
What weapons to select, what armour to indue.

XV

Youth ended, I shall try
My gain or loss thereby;
Leave the fire ashes, what survives is gold:
And I shall weigh the same,
Give life its praise or blame:
Young, all lay in dispute; I shall know, being old.

XVI

For, note when evening shuts,
A certain moment cuts
The deed off, calls the glory from the gray:
A whisper from the west
Shoots—"Add this to the rest,
Take it and try its worth: here dies another day."

XVII

So, still within this life,
Tho' lifted o'er its strife,
Let me discern, compare, pronounce at last,
"This rage was right i'the main,
That acquiescence vain:
The Future I may face now I have proved the Past."

XVIII

For more is not reserved
To man, with soul just nerved
To act to-morrow what he learns to-day:
Here, work enough to watch
The Master work, and catch
Hints of the proper craft, tricks of the tool's true play.

XIX

As it was better, youth
Should strive, thro' acts uncouth,
Toward making, than repose on aught found made:
        So, better, age, exempt
        From strife, should know, than tempt
Further. Thou waitedst age: wait death, nor be afraid!

XX

        Enough now, if the Right
        And Good and Infinite
Be named here, as thou callest thy hand thine own,
        With knowledge absolute,
        Subject to no dispute
From fools that crowded youth, nor let thee feel alone.

XXI

        Be there, for once and all,
        Severed great minds from small,
Announced to each his station in the Past!
        Was I, the world arraigned,
        Were they, my soul disdained,
Right? Let age speak the truth and give us peace at last!

XXII

Now, who shall arbitrate?
Ten men love what I hate,
Shun what I follow, slight what I receive;
Ten, who in ears and eyes
Match me: we all surmise,
They, this thing, and I, that: whom shall my soul believe?

XXIII

Not on the vulgar mass
Called "work," must sentence pass,
Things done, that took the eye and had the price;
O'er which, from level stand,
The low world laid its hand,
Found straight way to its mind, could value in a trice:

XXIV

But all, the world's coarse thumb
And finger failed to plumb,
So passed in making up the main account:
All instincts immature,
All purposes unsure,
That weighed not as his work, yet swelled the man's amount:

XXV

Thoughts hardly to be packed
Into a narrow act,
Fancies that broke thro' language and escaped:
All I could never be,
All, men ignored in me,
This, I was worth to God, whose wheel the pitcher shaped.

XXVI

Ay, note that Potter's wheel,
That metaphor! and feel
Why time spins fast, why passive lies our clay,—
Thou, to whom fools propound,
When the wine makes its round,
"Since life fleets, all is change; the Past gone, seize to-day!"

XXVII

Fool! All that is, at all,
Lasts ever, past recall;
Earth changes, but thy soul and God stand sure:
What entered into thee,
That was, is, and shall be:
Time's wheel runs back or stops: Potter and clay endure.

XXVIII

He fixed thee mid this dance
Of plastic circumstance,
This Present, thou forsooth, wouldst fain arrest:
Machinery just meant
To give thy soul its bent,
Try thee and turn thee forth, sufficiently impressed.

XXIX

What tho' the earlier grooves
Which ran the laughing loves
Around thy base, no longer pause and press?
What tho' about thy rim,
Scull-things in order grim
Grow out, in graver mood, obey the sterner stress?

XXX

Look not thou down but up!
To uses of a cup
The festal board, lamp's flash and trumpet's peal,
The new wine's foaming flow,
The Master's lips a-glow!
Thou, heaven's consummate cup, what needst thou with earth's wheel?

XXXI

But I need, now as then,
Thee, God, who mouldest men!
And since, not even while the whirl was worst,
Did I,—to the wheel of life
With shapes and colours rife,
Bound dizzily,—mistake my end, to slake Thy thirst.

XXXII

So take and use Thy work,
Amend what flaws may lurk,
What strain o' the stuff, what warpings past the aim!
My times be in Thy hand!
Perfect the cup as planned!
Let age approve of youth, and death complete the same!

A GRAMMARIAN'S FUNERAL

SHORTLY AFTER THE REVIVAL OF LEARNING IN EUROPE

Let us begin and carry up this corpse,
  Singing together.
Leave we the common crofts, the vulgar thorpes,
  Each in its tether
Sleeping safe on the bosom of the plain,
  Cared-for till cock-crow:
Look out if yonder be not day again
  Rimming the rock-row!
That's the appropriate country; there, man's thought,
  Rarer, intenser,
Self-gathered for an outbreak, as it ought,
  Chafes in the censer.
Leave we the unlettered plain its herd and crop;
  Seek we sepulture
On a tall mountain, citied to the top,
  Crowded with culture!
All the peaks soar, but one the rest excels;
  Clouds overcome it;
No! yonder sparkle is the citadel's
  Circling its summit.
Thither our path lies; wind we up the heights:
  Wait ye the warning?
Our low life was the level's and the night's:
  He's for the morning.

Step to a tune, square chests, erect each head,
'Ware the beholders!
This is our master, famous calm and dead,
Borne on our shoulders.

Sleep, crop and herd! sleep, darkling thorpe and croft,
Safe from the weather!
He, whom we convoy to his grave aloft,
Singing together,
He was a man born with thy face and throat,
Lyric Apollo!
Long he lived nameless: how should spring take note
Winter would follow?
Till lo, the little touch, and youth was gone!
Cramped and diminished,
Moaned he, "New measures, other feet anon!
My dance is finished?"
No, that's the world's way; (keep the mountain-side,
Make for the city!)
He knew the signal, and stepped on with pride
Over men's pity;
Left play for work, and grappled with the world
Bent on escaping:
"What's in the scroll," quoth he, "thou keepest furled?
Show me their shaping,
Theirs who most studied man, the bard and sage,—
Give!"—So, he gowned him,
Straight got by heart that book to its last page:
Learned, we found him.

Yea, but we found him bald too, eyes like lead,
        Accents uncertain:
"Time to taste life," another would have said,
        "Up with the curtain!"
This man said rather, "Actual life comes next?
        Patience a moment!
Grant I have mastered learning's crabbed text,
        Still there's the comment.
Let me know all! Prate not of most or least,
        Painful or easy!
Even to the crumbs I'd fain eat up the feast,
        Ay, nor feel queasy."
Oh, such a life as he resolved to live,
        When he had learned it,
When he had gathered all books had to give!
        Sooner, he spurned it.
Image the whole, then execute the parts—
        Fancy the fabric
Quite, ere you build, ere steel strikes fire from quartz,
        Ere mortar dab brick.

(Here's the town-gate reached; there's the market-place
        Gaping before us.)
Yea, this in him was the peculiar grace
        (Hearten our chorus!)
That before living he'd learn how to live—
        No end to learning:
Earn the means first—God surely will contrive
        Use for our earning.

Others mistrust and say, "But time escapes!
    Live now or never!"
He said, "What's time? Leave Now for dogs and apes!
    Man has Forever."
Back to his book then: deeper drooped his head:
    Calculus racked him:
Leaden before, his eyes grew dross of lead:
    Tussis attacked him.
"Now, master, take a little rest!"—not he!
    (Caution redoubled!
Step two abreast, the way winds narrowly!)
    Not a whit troubled,
Back to his studies, fresher than at first,
    Fierce as a dragon
He (soul-hydroptic with a sacred thirst)
    Sucked at the flagon.
Oh, if we draw a circle premature,
    Heedless of far gain,
Greedy for quick returns of profit, sure
    Bad is our bargain!
Was it not great? did not he throw on God
    (He loves the burthen)—
God's task to make the heavenly period
    Perfect the earthen?
Did not he magnify the mind, show clear
    Just what it all meant?
He would not discount life, as fools do here,
    Paid by instalment.

He ventured neck or nothing—heaven's success
Found, or earth's failure:
"Wilt thou trust death or not?" He answered "Yes!
Hence with life's pale lure!"
That low man seeks a little thing to do,
Sees it and does it:
This high man, with a great thing to pursue,
Dies ere he knows it.
That low man goes on adding one to one,
His hundred's soon hit:
This high man, aiming at a million,
Misses an unit.
That, has the world here—should he need the next,
Let the world mind him!
This, throws himself on God, and unperplexed
Seeking shall find Him.
So, with the throttling hands of death at strife,
Ground he at grammar;
Still, thro' the rattle, parts of speech were rife:
While he could stammer
He settled *Hoti's* business—let it be!—
Properly based *Oun*—
Gave us the doctrine of the enclitic *De,*
Dead from the waist down.
Well, here's the platform, here's the proper place:
Hail to your purlieus,
All ye highfliers of the feathered race,
Swallows and curlews:

Here's the top-peak; the multitude below
	Live, for they can, there:
This man decided not to Live, but Know—
	Bury this man there?
Here—here's his place, where meteors shoot, clouds form,
	Lightnings are loosened,
Stars come and go! Let joy break with the storm,
	Peace let the dew send!
Lofty designs must close in like effects:
	Loftily lying,
Leave him—still loftier than the world suspects,
	Living and dying.

ANDREA DEL SARTO
(CALLED "THE FAULTLESS PAINTER")

But do not let us quarrel any more,
No, my Lucrezia! bear with me for once:
Sit down and all shall happen as you wish.
You turn your face, but does it bring your heart?
I'll work then for your friend's friend, never fear.
Treat his own subject after his own way,
Fix his own time, accept too his own price,
And shut the money into this small hand
When next it takes mine. Will it? tenderly?
Oh, I'll content him,—but to-morrow, Love!
I often am much wearier than you think,
This evening more than usual: and it seems
As if—forgive now—should you let me sit
Here by the window, with your hand in mine,
And look a half-hour forth on Fiesole,
Both of one mind, as married people use,
Quietly, quietly the evening through,
I might get up to-morrow to my work
Cheerful and fresh as ever. Let us try.
To-morrow, how you shall be glad for this!
Your soft hand is a woman of itself,
And mine the man's bared breast she curls inside.
Don't count the time lost, neither; you must serve
For each of the five pictures we require:
It saves a model. So! keep looking so—

My serpentining beauty, rounds on rounds!
—How could you ever prick those perfect ears,
Even to put the pearl there! oh, so sweet—
My face, my moon, my everybody's moon.
Which everybody looks on and calls his,
And, I suppose, is looked on by in turn,
While she looks—no one's: very dear, no less.
You smile? why, there's my picture ready made,
There's what we painters call our harmony!
A common grayness silvers everything,—
All in a twilight, you and I alike
—You, at the point of your first pride in me
(That's gone, you know)—but I, at every point;
My youth, my hope, my art, being all toned down
To yonder sober pleasant Fiesole.
There's the bell clinking from the chapel-top;
That length of convent-wall across the way
Holds the trees safer, huddled more inside;
The last monk leaves the garden; days decrease,
And autumn grows, autumn in everything.
Eh? the whole seems to fall into a shape,
As if I saw alike my work and self
And all that I was born to be and do,
A twilight-piece. Love, we are in God's hand.
How strange now, looks the life he makes us lead;
So free we seem, so fettered fast we are!
I feel he laid the fetter: let it lie!
This chamber for example—turn your head—
All that's behind us! You don't understand

Nor care to understand about my art,
But you can hear at least when people speak:
And that cartoon, the second from the door
—It is the thing, Love! so such things should be—
Behold Madonna!—I am bold to say.
I can do with my pencil what I know,
What I see, what at bottom of my heart
I wish for, if I ever wish so deep—
Do easily, too—when I say, perfectly,
I do not boast, perhaps: yourself are judge,
Who listened to the Legate's talk last week;
And just as much they used to say in France.
At any rate 'tis easy, all of it!
No sketches first, no studies, that's long past:
I do what many dream of, all their lives,
—Dream? strive to do, and agonize to do,
And fail in doing. I could count twenty such
On twice your fingers, and not leave this town,
Who strive—you don't know how the others strive
To paint a little thing like that you smeared
Carelessly passing with your robes afloat,—
Yet do much less, so much less. Someone says,
(I know his name, no matter)—so much less!
Well, less is more, Lucrezia: I am judged.
There burns a truer light of God in them,
In their vexed beating stuffed and stopped-up brain,
Heart, or whate'er else, than goes on to prompt
This low-pulsed forthright craftsman's hand of mine.
Their works drop groundward, but themselves, I know,

Reach many a time a heaven that's shut to me,
Enter and take their place there sure enough,
Tho' they come back and cannot tell the world.
My works are nearer heaven, but I sit here.
The sudden blood of these men! at a word—
Praise them, it boils, or blame them, it boils too.
I, painting from myself and to myself,
Know what I do, am unmoved by men's blame
Or their praise either. Somebody remarks
Morello's outline there is wrongly traced,
His hue mistaken; what of that? or else,
Rightly traced and well ordered; what of that?
Speak as they please, what does the mountain care?
Ah, but a man's reach should exceed his grasp,
Or what's a heaven for? All is silver-gray,
Placid and perfect with my art: the worse!
I know both what I want and what might gain,
And yet how profitless to know, to sigh
"Had I been two, another and myself,
Our head would have o'erlooked the world!" No doubt.
Yonder's a work now, of that famous youth
The Urbinate who died five years ago.
('Tis copied, George Vasari sent it me.)
Well, I can fancy how he did it all,
Pouring his soul, with kings and popes to see,
Reaching, that heaven might so replenish him,
Above and thro' his art—for it gives way;
That arm is wrongly put—and there again—
A fault to pardon in the drawing's lines,

Its body, so to speak: its soul is right,
He means right—that, a child may understand.
Still, what an arm! and I could alter it:
But all the play, the insight and the stretch—
Out of me, out of me! And wherefore out?
Had you enjoined them on me, given me soul,
We might have risen to Rafael, I and you!
Nay, Love, you did give all I asked, I think—
More than I merit, yes, by many times.
But had you—oh, with the same perfect brow,
And perfect eyes, and more than perfect mouth,
And the low voice my soul hears, as a bird
The fowler's pipe, and follows to the snare—
Had you, with these the same, but brought a mind!
Some women do so. Had the mouth there urged
"God and the glory! never care for gain.
The present by the future, what is that?
Live for fame, side by side with Agnolo!
Rafael is waiting: up to God, all three!"
I might have done it for you. So it seems:
Perhaps not. All is as God over-rules.
Beside, incentives come from the soul's self;
The rest avail not. Why do I need you?
What wife had Rafael, or has Agnolo?
In this world, who can do a thing, will not;
And who would do it, cannot, I perceive:
Yet the will's somewhat—somewhat, too, the power—
And thus we half-men struggle. At the end,
God, I conclude, compensates, punishes.

'Tis safer for me, if the award be strict,
That I am something underrated here,
Poor this long while, despised, to speak the truth.
I dared not, do you know, leave home all day,
For fear of chancing on the Paris lords.
The best is when they pass and look aside;
But they speak sometimes; I must bear it all.
Well may they speak. That Francis, that first time,
And that long festal year at Fontainebleau!
I surely then could sometimes leave the ground,
Put on the glory, Rafael's daily wear,
In that humane great monarch's golden look,—
One finger in his beard or twisted curl
Over his mouth's good mark that made the smile.
One arm, about my shoulder, round my neck,
The jingle of his gold chain in my ear,
I painting proudly with his breath on me,
All his court round him, seeing with his eyes.
Such frank French eyes, and such a fire of souls
Profuse, my hand kept plying by those hearts,—
And, best of all, this, this, this face beyond,
This in the background, waiting on my work,
To crown the issue with a last reward!
A good tune, was it not, my kingly days?
And had you not grown restless...but I know—
'Tis done and past; 'twas right, my instinct said;
Too live the life grew, golden and not gray:
And I'm the weak-eyed bat no sun should tempt
Out of the grange whose four walls make his world,

How could it end in any other way?
You called me, and I came home to your heart,
The triumph was—to reach and stay there; since
I reached it ere the triumph, what is lost?
Let my hands frame your face in your hair's gold,
You beautiful Lucrezia that are mine!
"Rafael did this, Andrea painted that;
The Roman's is the better when you pray,
But still the other's Virgin was his wife—"
Men will excuse me. I am glad to judge
Both pictures in your presence; clearer grows
My better fortune, I resolve to think.
For, do you know, Lucrezia, as God lives,
Said one day Agnolo, his very self,
To Rafael...I have known it all these years...
(When the young man was flaming out his thoughts
Upon a palace-wall for Rome to see,
Too lifted up in heart because of it)
"Friend, there's a certain sorry little scrub
Goes up and down our Florence, none cares how,
Who, were he set to plan and execute
As you are, pricked on by your popes and kings,
Would bring the sweat into that brow of yours!"
To Rafael's!—And indeed the arm is wrong.
I hardly dare ... yet, only you to see,
Give the chalk here—quick, thus the line should go!
Ay, but the soul! he's Rafael! rub it out!
Still, all I care for, if he spoke the truth,
(What he? why, who but Michel Agnolo?

Do you forget already words like those?)
If really there was such a chance so lost,—
Is, whether you're—not grateful—but more pleased.
Well, let me think so. And you smile indeed!
This hour has been an hour! Another smile?
If you would sit thus by me every night
I should work better, do you comprehend?
I mean that I should earn more, give you more.
See, it is settled dusk now; there's a star;
Morello's gone, the watch-lights show the wall,
The cue-owls speak the name we call them by.
Come from the window, Love,—come in, at last,
Inside the melancholy little house
We built to be so gay with. God is just.
King Francis may forgive me: oft at nights
When I look up from painting, eyes tired out,
The walls become illumined, brick from brick
Distinct, instead of mortar, fierce, bright gold,
That gold of his I did cement them with!
Let us but love each other. Must you go?
That Cousin here again? he waits outside?
Must see you—you, and not with me? Those loans?
More gaming debts to pay? you smiled for that?
Well, let smiles buy me! have you more to spend?
While hand and eye and something of a heart
Are left me, work's my ware, and what's it worth?
I'll pay my fancy. Only let me sit
The gray remainder of the evening out,
Idle, you call it, and muse perfectly

How I could paint, were I but back in France,
One picture, just one more—the Virgin's face,
Not yours this time! I want you at my side
To hear them—that is, Michel Agnolo—
Judge all I do and tell you of its worth.
Will you? To-morrow, satisfy your friend.
I take the subjects for his corridor,
Finish the portrait out of hand—there, there,
And throw him in another thing or two
If he demurs; the whole should prove enough
To pay for this same Cousin's freak. Beside,
What's better and what's all I care about,
Get you the thirteen scudi for the ruff!
Love, does that please you? Ah, but what does he,
The Cousin! what does he to please you more?
I am grown peaceful as old age to-night.
I regret little, I would change still less.
Since there my past life lies, why alter it?
The very wrong to Francis!—it is true
I took his coin, was tempted and complied,
And built this house and sinned, and all is said
My father and my mother died of want.
Well, had I riches of my own? you see
How one gets rich! Let each one bear his lot.
They were born poor, lived poor, and poor they died:
And I have laboured somewhat in my time
And not been paid profusely. Some good son
Paint my two hundred pictures—let him try!
No doubt, there's something strikes a balance. Yes,

You love me quite enough, it seems to-night.
This must suffice me here. What would one have?
In heaven, perhaps, new chances, one more chance—
Four great walls in the New Jerusalem,
Meted on each side by the angel's reed,
For Leonard, Rafael, Agnolo, and me
To cover—the three first without a wife,
While I have mine! So—still they overcome
Because there's still Lucrezia,—as I choose.

Again the Cousin's whistle! Go, my Love.

CALIBAN UPON SETEBOS

OR, NATURAL THEOLOGY IN THE ISLAND

"Thou thoughtest that I was altogether such an one as thyself."

['Will sprawl, now that the heat of day is best,
Flat on his belly in the pit's much mire,
With elbows wide, fists clenched to prop his chin,
And, while he kicks both feet in the cool slush,
And feels about his spine small eft-things course,
Run in and out each arm, and make him laugh:
And while above his head a pompion-plant,
Coating the cave-top as a brow its eye,
Creeps down to touch and tickle hair and beard,
And now a flower drops with a bee inside,
And now a fruit to snap at, catch and crunch,—
He looks out o'er yon sea which sunbeams cross
And recross till they weave a spider-web,
(Meshes of fire, some great fish breaks at times)
And talks, to his own self, howe'er he please,
Touching that other, whom his dam called God.
Because to talk about Him, vexes—ha,
Could He but know! and time to vex is now,
When talk is safer than in winter-time.
Moreover Prosper and Miranda sleep
In confidence, he drudges at their task,
And it is good to cheat the pair, and gibe,
Letting the rank tongue blossom into speech.]

Setebos, Setebos, and Setebos!
'Thinketh, He dwelleth i' the cold o' the moon.

'Thinketh He made it, with the sun to match,
But not the stars; the stars came otherwise;
Only made clouds, winds, meteors, such as that:
Also this isle, what lives and grows thereon,
And snaky sea which rounds and ends the same.

'Thinketh, it came of being ill at ease:
He hated that He cannot change His cold,
Nor cure its ache. 'Hath spied an icy fish
That longed to 'scape the rock-stream where she lived,
And thaw herself within the lukewarm brine
O' the lazy sea her stream thrusts far amid,
A crystal spike 'twixt two warm walls of wave;
Only, she ever sickened, found repulse
At the other kind of water, not her life,
(Green-dense and dim-delicious, bred o' the sun)
Flounced back from bliss she was not born to breathe,
And in her old bounds buried her despair,
Hating and loving warmth alike: so He.

'Thinketh, He made thereat the sun, this isle,
Trees and the fowls here, beast and creeping thing.
Yon otter, sleek-wet, black, lithe as a leech;
Yon auk, one fire-eye in a ball of foam,
That floats and feeds; a certain badger brown,
He hath watched hunt with that slant white-wedge eye

By moonlight; and the pie with the long tongue
That pricks deep into oakwarts for a worm,
And says a plain word when she finds her prize,
But will not eat the ants; the ants themselves
That build a wall of seeds and settled stalks
About their hole—He made all these and more,
Made all we see, and us, in spite: how else?
He could not, Himself, make a second self
To be His mate: as well have made Himself:
He would not make what He mislikes or slights,
An eyesore to Him, or not worth His pains;
But did, in envy, listlessness, or sport,
Make what Himself would fain, in a manner, be—
Weaker in most points, stronger in a few,
Worthy, and yet mere playthings all the while,
Things He admires and mocks too,—that is it!
Because, so brave, so better tho' they be,
It nothing skills if He begin to plague.
Look now, I melt a gourd-fruit into mash,
Add honeycomb and pods, I have perceived,
Which bite like finches when they bill and kiss,—
Then, when froth rises bladdery, drink up all,
Quick, quick, till maggots scamper thro' my brain;
Last, throw me on my back i'the seeded thyme.
And wanton, wishing I were born a bird.
Put case, unable to be what I wish,
I yet could make a live bird out of clay:
Would not I take clay, pinch my Caliban
Able to fly?—for there, see, he hath wings,

And great comb like the hoopoe's to admire,
And there, a sting to do his foes offence,
There, and I will that he begin to live,
Fly to yon rock-top, nip me off the horns
Of grigs high up that make the merry din,
Saucy thro' their veined wings, and mind me not.
In which feat, if his leg snapped, brittle clay,
And he lay stupid-like,—why, I should laugh;
And if he, spying me, should fall to weep,
Beseech me to be good, repair his wrong,
Bid his poor leg smart less or grow again,—
Well, as the chance were, this might take or else
Not take my fancy: I might hear his cry,
And give the mankin three sound legs for one,
Or pluck the other off, leave him like an egg,
And lessoned he was mine and merely clay.
Were this no pleasure, lying in the thyme,
Drinking the mash, with brain become alive,
Making and marring clay at will? So He.

'Thinketh such shows nor right nor wrong in Him,
Nor kind, nor cruel: He is strong and Lord.
'Am strong myself compared to yonder crabs
That march now from the mountain to the sea;
'Let twenty pass, and stone the twenty-first,
Loving not, hating not, just choosing so.
'Say, the first straggler that boasts purple spots
Shall join the file, one pincer twisted off;
'Say, this bruised fellow shall receive a worm.

And two worms he whose nippers end in red:
As it likes me each time, I do: so He.

Well then, 'supposeth He is good i'the main,
Placable if His mind and ways were guessed,
But rougher than His handiwork, be sure!
Oh, He hath made things worthier than Himself,
And envieth that, so helped, such things do more
Than He who made them! What consoles but this?
That they, unless thro' Him, do naught at all,
And must submit: what other use in things?
'Hath cut a pipe of pithless elder-joint
That, blown through, gives exact the scream o' the jay
When from her wing you twitch the feathers blue;
Sound this, and little birds that hate the jay
Flock within stone's throw, glad their foe is hurt:
Put case such pipe could prattle and boast forsooth
"I catch the birds, I am the crafty thing,
I make the cry my maker cannot make
With his great round mouth; he must blow thro' mine!"
Would not I smash it with my foot? So He.

But wherefore rough, why cold and ill at ease?
Aha, that is a question! Ask, for that,
What knows,—the something over Setebos
That made Him, or He, may be, found and fought,
Worsted, drove off and did to nothing, perchance.
There may be something quiet o'er His head,
Out of His reach, that feels nor joy nor grief,

Since both derive from weakness in some way.
I joy because the quails come; would not joy
Could I bring quails here when I have a mind:
This Quiet, all it hath a mind to, doth.
'Esteemeth stars the outposts of its couch,
But never spends much thought nor care that way.
It may look up, work up,—the worse for those
It works on! 'Careth but for Setebos
The many-handed as a cuttle-fish,
Who, making Himself feared thro' what He does,
Looks up, first, and perceives he cannot soar
To what is quiet and hath happy life;
Next looks down here, and out of very spite
Makes this a bauble-world to ape yon real,
These good things to match those as hips do grapes.
'Tis solace making baubles, ay, and sport.
Himself peeped late, eyed Prosper at his books
Careless and lofty, lord now of the isle:
Vexed, 'stitched a book of broad leaves, arrow-shaped,
Wrote thereon, he knows what, prodigious words;
Has peeled a wand and called it by a name;
Weareth at whiles for an enchanter's robe
The eyed skin of a supple oncelot;
And hath an ounce sleeker than youngling mole,
A four-legged serpent he makes cower and couch,
Now snarl, now hold its breath and mind his eye,
And saith she is Miranda and my wife:
'Keeps for his Ariel a tall pouch-bill crane
He bids go wade for fish and straight disgorge;

Also a sea-beast, lumpish, which he snared,
Blinded the eyes of, and brought somewhat tame,
And split its toe-webs, and now pens the drudge
In a hole o' the rock, and calls him Caliban;
A bitter heart that bides its time and bites.
'Plays thus at being Prosper in a way,
Taketh his mirth with make-believes: so He.

His dam held that the Quiet made all things
Which Setebos vexed only: 'holds not so.
Who made them weak, meant weakness He might vex.
Had He meant other, while His hand was in,
Why not make horny eyes no thorn could prick,
Or plate my scalp with bone against the snow,
Or overscale my flesh 'neath joint and joint,
Like an orc's armour? Ay,—so spoil His sport!
He is the One now: only He doth all.

'Saith, He may like, perchance, what profits Him.
Ay, himself loves what does him good; but why?
'Gets good no otherwise. This blinded beast
Loves whoso places flesh-meat on his nose.
But, had he eyes, would want no help, but hate
Or love, just as it liked him: He hath eyes.
Also it pleaseth Setebos to work,
Use all His hands, and exercise much craft,
By no means for the love of what is worked.
'Tasteth, himself, no finer good i'the world
When all goes right, in this safe summer-time,

And he wants little, hungers, aches not much,
Than trying what to do with wit and strength.
'Falls to make something; 'piled yon pile of turfs,
And squared and stuck there squares of soft white chalk,
And, with a fish-tooth, scratched a moon on each,
And set up endwise certain spikes of tree,
And crowned the whole with a sloth's skull a-top,
Found dead i'the woods, too hard for one to kill.
No use at all i'the work, for work's sole sake;
'Shall some day knock it down again: so He.

'Saith He is terrible: watch His feats in proof!
One hurricane will spoil six good months' hope.
He hath a spite against me, that I know.
Just as He favours Prosper, who knows why?
So it is, all the same, as well I find.
'Wove wattles half the winter, fenced them firm
With stone and stake to stop she-tortoises
Crawling to lay their eggs here: well, one wave,
Feeling the foot of Him upon its neck,
Gaped as a snake does, lolled out its large tongue,
And licked the whole labour flat; so much for spite!
'Saw a ball flame down late (yonder it lies)
Where, half an hour before, I slept i'the shade:
Often they scatter sparkles: there is force!
'Dug up a newt He may have envied once
And turned to stone, shut up inside a stone.
Please Him and hinder this?—What Prosper does?
Aha, if he would tell me how! Not he!

There is the sport: discover how or die!
All need not die, for of the things o'the isle
Some flee afar, some dive, some run up trees;
Those at His mercy,—why, they please Him most
When...when...well, never try the same way twice!
Repeat what act has pleased, He may grow wroth.
You must not know His ways, and play Him off,
Sure of the issue. 'Doth the like himself:
'Spareth a squirrel that it nothing fears
But steals the nut from underneath my thumb,
And when I threat, bites stoutly in defence:
'Spareth an urchin that contrariwise,
Curls up into a ball, pretending death
For fright at my approach: the two ways please.
But what would move my choler more than this,
That either creature counted on its life
To-morrow, next day and all days to come,
Saying forsooth in the inmost of its heart,
"Because he did so yesterday with me,
And otherwise with such another brute,
So must he do henceforth and always." Ay?
'Would teach the reasoning couple what "must" means!
'Doth as he likes, or wherefore Lord? So He.

'Conceiveth all things will continue thus,
And we shall have to live in fear of Him
So long as He lives, keeps His strength: no change,
If He have done His best, make no new world
To please Him more, so leave off watching this,—

If He surprise not even the Quiet's self
Some strange day,—or, suppose, grow into it
As grubs grow butterflies: else, here are we,
And there is He, and nowhere help at all.

'Believeth with the life the pain shall stop.
His dam held different, that after death
He both plagued enemies and feasted friends:
Idly! He doth His worst in this our life,
Giving just respite lest we die thro' pain,
Saving last pain for worst,—with which, an end.
Meanwhile, the best way to escape His Ire
Is, not to seem too happy. 'Sees, himself,
Yonder two flies, with purple films and pink,
Bask on the pompion-bell above: kills both.
'Sees two black painful beetles roll their ball
On head and tail as if to save their lives:
'Moves them the stick away they strive to clear.

Even so, 'would have him misconceive, suppose
This Caliban strives hard and ails no less,
And always, above all else, envies Him;
Wherefore he mainly dances on dark nights,
Moans in the sun, gets under holes to laugh,
And never speaks his mind save housed as now:
Outside, 'groans, curses. If He caught me here,
O'erheard this speech, and asked "What chucklest at?"
'Would to appease Him, cut a finger off,
Or of my three kid yearlings burn the best,

Or let the toothsome apples rot on tree,
Or push my tame beast for the orc to taste:
While myself lit a fire, and made a song
And sung it, "*What I hate, be consecrate*
To celebrate Thee and Thy state, no mate
For Thee; what see for envy in poor me?"
Hoping the while, since evils sometimes mend,
Warts rub away and sores are cured with slime,
That some strange day, will either the Quiet catch
And conquer Setebos, or likelier He
Decrepit may doze, doze, as good as die.

[What, what? A curtain o'er the world at once!
Crickets stop hissing; not a bird—or, yes,
There scuds His raven, that hath told Him all!
It was fool's play, this prattling! Ha! The wind
Shoulders the pillared dust, death's house o'the move,
And fast invading fires begin! White blaze—
A tree's head snaps—and there, there, there, there, there,
His thunder follows! Fool to gibe at Him!
So! 'Lieth flat and loveth Setebos!
'Maketh his teeth meet thro' his upper lip,
Will let those quails fly, will not eat this month
One little mess of whelks, so he may 'scape!]

"CHILDE ROLAND TO THE DARK TOWER CAME"

(See Edgar's song in "Lear.")

I

My first thought was, he lied in every word,
    That hoary cripple, with malicious eye
    Askance to watch the working of his lie
On mine, and mouth scarce able to afford
Suppression of the glee, that pursed and scored
    Its edge, at one more victim gained thereby.

II

What else should he be set for, with his staff?
    What, save to waylay with his lies, ensnare
    All travellers who might find him posted there,
And ask the road? I guessed what skull-like laugh
Would break, what crutch 'gin write my epitaph
    For pastime in the dusty thoroughfare,

III

If at his counsel I should turn aside
    Into that ominous tract which, all agree,
    Hides the Dark Tower. Yet acquiescingly
I did turn as he pointed: neither pride
Nor hope rekindling at the end descried.
    So much as gladness that some end might be.

IV

For, what with my whole world-wide wandering,
    What, with my search drawn out thro' years, my hope
    Dwindled into a ghost not fit to cope
With that obstreperous joy success would bring,—
I hardly tried now to rebuke the spring
    My heart made, finding failure in its scope.

V

As when a sick man very near to death
    Seems dead indeed, and feels begin and end
    The tears, and takes the farewell of each friend,
And hears one bid the other go, draw breath
Freelier outside, ("since all is o'er," he saith,
    "And the blow fallen no grieving can amend;")

VI

While some discuss if near the other graves
    Be room enough for this, and when a day
    Suits best for carrying the corpse away,
With care about the banners, scarves, and staves:
And still the man hears all, and only craves
    He may not shame such tender love and stay.

VII

Thus, I had so long suffered in this quest,
    Heard failure prophesied so oft, been writ
    So many times among "The Band"—to wit,
The knights who to the Dark Tower's search addressed
Their steps—that just to fail as they, seemed best,
    And all the doubt was now—should I be fit?

VIII

So, quiet as despair, I turned from him,
    That hateful cripple, out of his highway
    Into the path he pointed. All the day
Had been a dreary one at best, and dim
Was settling to its close, yet shot one grim
    Red leer to see the plain catch its estray.

IX

For mark! no sooner was I fairly found
    Pledged to the plain, after a pace or two,
    Than, pausing to throw backward a last view
O'er the safe road, 'twas gone; gray plain all round:
Nothing but plain to the horizon's bound,
    I might go on; naught else remained to do.

X

So, on I went. I think I never saw
    Such starved ignoble nature; nothing throve:
    For flowers—as well expect a cedar grove!
But cockle, spurge, according to their law
Might propagate their kind, with none to awe,
    You'd think; a burr had been a treasure trove.

XI

No! penury, inertness, and grimace,
    In some strange sort, were the land's portion. "See
    Or shut your eyes," said Nature peevishly,
"It nothing skills: I cannot help my case:
'Tis the Last Judgment's fire must cure this place,
    Calcine its clods and set my prisoners free."

XII

If there pushed any ragged thistle-stalk
    Above its mates, the head was chopped; the bents
    Were jealous else. What made those holes and rents
In the dock's harsh swarth leaves, bruised as to balk
All hope of greenness? 'tis a brute must walk
    Pashing their life out, with a brute's intents.

XIII

As for the grass, it grew as scant as hair
    In leprosy; thin dry blades pricked the mud
    Which underneath looked kneaded up with blood.
One stiff blind horse, his every bone a-stare,
Stood stupefied, however he came there:
    Thrust out past service from the devil's stud!

XIV

Alive? he might be dead for aught I know,
    With that red gaunt and colloped neck a-strain,
    And shut eyes underneath the rusty mane;
Seldom went such grotesqueness with such woe;
I never saw a brute I hated so;
    He must be wicked to deserve such pain.

XV

I shut my eyes and turned them on my heart.
    As a man calls for wine before he fights,
    I asked one draught of earlier, happier sights,
Ere fitly I could hope to play my part.
Think first, fight afterwards—the soldier's art:
    One taste of the old time sets all to rights.

XVI

Not it! I fancied Cuthbert's reddening face
    Beneath its garniture of curly gold,
    Dear fellow, till I almost felt him fold
An arm in mine to fix me to the place,
That way he used. Alas, one night's disgrace!
    Out went my heart's new fire and left it cold.

XVII

Giles then, the soul of honour—there he stands
    Frank as ten years ago when knighted first.
    What honest man should dare (he said) he durst.
Good—but the scene shifts—faugh! what hangman hands
Pin to his breast a parchment? His own bands
    Read it. Poor traitor, spit upon and curst!

XVIII

Better this present than a past like that;
    Back therefore to my darkening path again!
    No sound, no sight so far as eye could strain.
Will the night send a howlet or a bat?
I asked: when something on the dismal flat
    Came to arrest my thoughts and change their train.

XIX

A sudden little river crossed my path
As unexpected as a serpent comes.
No sluggish tide congenial to the glooms;
This, as it frothed by, might have been a bath
For the fiend's glowing hoof—to see the wrath
Of its black eddy bespate with flakes and spumes.

XX

So petty, yet so spiteful! All along,
Low scrubby alders kneeled down over it;
Drenched willows flung them headlong in a fit
Of mute despair, a suicidal throng:
The river which had done them all the wrong,
Whate'er that was, rolled by, deterred no whit.

XXI

Which, while I forded,—good saints, how I feared
To set my foot upon a dead man's cheek,
Each step, or feel the spear I thrust to seek
For hollows, tangled in his hair or beard!
—It may have been a water-rat I speared,
But, ugh! it sounded like a baby's shriek.

XXII

Glad was I when I reached the other bank.
    Now for a better country. Vain presage!
    Who were the strugglers, what war did they wage
Whose savage trample thus could pad the dank
Soil to a plash? Toads in a poisoned tank,
    Or wild cats in a red-hot iron cage—

XXIII

The fight must so have seemed in that fell cirque.
    What penned them there, with all the plain, to choose?
    No foot-print leading to that horrid mews,
None out of it. Mad brewage set to work
Their brains, no doubt, like galley-slaves the Turk
    Pits for his pastime, Christians against Jews.

XXIV

And more than that—a furlong on—why, there!
    What bad use was that engine deg. for, that wheel,
    Or brake, not wheel—that harrow fit to reel
Men's bodies out like silk? with all the air
Of Tophet's tool, on earth left unaware,
    Or brought to sharpen its rusty teeth of steel.

XXV

Then came a bit of stubbed ground, once a wood,
    Next a marsh, it would seem, and now mere earth
    Desperate and done with; (so a fool finds mirth,
Makes a thing and then mars it, till his mood
Changes, and off he goes!) within a rood—
    Bog, clay, and rubble, sand, and stark black dearth.

XXVI

Now blotches rankling, coloured gay and grim,
    Now patches where some leanness of the soil's
    Broke into moss or substances like boils;
Then came some palsied oak, a cleft in him
Like a distorted mouth that splits its rim
    Gaping at death, and dies while it recoils.

XXVII

And just as far as ever from the end,
    Naught in the distance but the evening, naught
    To point my footstep further! At the thought,
A great black bird, Apollyon's Bosom-friend,
Sailed past, nor beat his wide wing dragon-penned
    That brushed my cap—perchance the guide I sought.

XXVIII

For, looking up, aware I somehow grew,
    'Spite of the dusk, the plain had given place
    All round to mountains—with such name to grace
Mere ugly heights and heaps now stolen in view.
How thus they had surprised me,—solve it, you!
    How to get from them was no clearer case.

XXIX

Yet half I seemed to recognize some trick
    Of mischief happened to me, Gods knows when—
    In a bad dream, perhaps. Here ended, then,
Progress this way. When, in the very nick
Of giving up, one time more, came a click
    As when a trap shuts—you're inside the den.

XXX

Burningly it came on me all at once,
    This was the place! those two hills on the right,
    Crouched like two bulls locked horn in horn in fight;
While, to the left, a tall scalped mountain...Dunce,
Dotard, a-dozing at the very nonce,
    After a life spent training for the sight!

XXXI

What in the midst lay but the Tower itself?
    The round squat turret, blind as the fool's heart,
    Built of brown stone, without a counterpart
In the whole world. The tempest's mocking elf
Points to the shipman thus the unseen shelf
    He strikes on, only when the timbers start.

XXXII

Not see? because of night perhaps?—why, day
    Came back again for that! before it left,
    The dying sunset kindled thro' a cleft:
The hills, like giants at a hunting, lay,
Chin upon hand, to see the game at bay,
    "Now stab and end the creature—to the heft!"

XXXIII

Not hear? when noise was everywhere! it tolled
    Increasing like a bell. Names in my ears,
    Of all the lost adventurers my peers,—
How such a one was strong, and such was bold,
And such was fortunate, yet each of old
    Lost, lost! one moment knelled the woe of years.

XXXIV

There they stood, ranged along the hillsides, met
To view the last of me, a living frame
For one more picture! in a sheet of flame
I saw them and I knew them all. And yet
Dauntless the slug-horn to my lips I set,
And blew. "*Childe Roland to the Dark Tower came.*"

AN EPISTLE

CONTAINING THE STRANGE MEDICAL EXPERIENCE OF KARSHISH, THE ARAB PHYSICIAN

Karshish, the picker up of learning's crumbs,
The not incurious in God's handiwork
(This man's flesh he hath admirably made,
Blown like a bubble, kneaded like a paste,
To coop up and keep down on earth a space
That puff of vapour from his mouth, man's soul)
—To Abib, all sagacious in our art,
Breeder in me of what poor skill I boast,
Like me inquisitive how pricks and cracks
Befall the flesh through too much stress and strain,
Whereby the wily vapour fain would slip
Back and rejoin its source before the term,—
And aptest in contrivance (under God)
To baffle it by deftly stopping such—
The vagrant Scholar to his Sage at home
Sends greeting (health and knowledge, fame with peace)
Three samples of true snake-stone—rarer still,
One of the other sort, the melon-shaped,
(But fitter, pounded fine, for charms than drugs)
And writeth now the twenty-second time.

My journeyings were brought to Jericho:
Thus I resume. Who studious in our art
Shall count a little labour unrepaid?
I have shed sweat enough, left flesh and bone
On many a flinty furlong of this land.
Also, the country-side is all on fire
With rumours of a marching hitherward:
Some say Vespasian cometh, some, his son.
A black lynx snarled and pricked a tufted ear:
Lust of my blood inflamed his yellow balls:
I cried and threw my staff and he was gone.
Twice have the robbers stripped and beaten me,
And once a town declared me for a spy;
But at the end, I reach Jerusalem,
Since this poor covert where I pass the night,
This Bethany, lies scarce the distance thence
A man with plague-sores at the third degree
Runs till he drops down dead. Thou laughest here!
'Sooth, it elates me, thus reposed and safe,
To void the stuffing of my travel-scrip
And share with thee whatever Jewry yields.
A viscid choler is observable
In tertians, I was nearly bold to say;
And falling-sickness hath a happier cure
Than our school wots of: there's a spider here
Weaves no web, watches on the ledge of tombs,
Sprinkled with mottles on an ash-gray back;
Take five and drop them...but who knows his mind,
The Syrian run-a-gate I trust this to?

His service payeth me a sublimate
Blown up his nose to help the ailing eye.
Best wait: I reach Jerusalem at morn,
There set in order my experiences,
Gather what most deserves, and give thee all—
Or I might add, Judæa's gum-tragacanth
Scales off in purer flakes, shines clearer-grained,
Cracks 'twixt the pestle and the porphyry.
In fine exceeds our produce. Scalp-disease
Confounds me, crossing so with leprosy:
Thou hadst admired one sort I gained at Zoar—
But zeal outruns discretion. Here I end.

Yet stay! my Syrian blinketh gratefully,
Protested his devotion is my price—
Suppose I write, what harms not, tho' he steal?
I half resolve to tell thee, yet I blush,
What set me off a-writing first of all.
An itch I had, a sting to write, a tang!
For, be it this town's barrenness—or else
The man had something in the look of him—
His case has struck me far more than 'tis worth.
So, pardon if—(lest presently I lose,
In the great press of novelty at hand,
The care and pains this somehow stole from me)
I bid thee take the thing while fresh in mind.

Almost in sight—for, wilt thou have the truth?
The very man is gone from me but now,
Whose ailment is the subject of discourse.
Thus then, and let thy better wit help all!

'Tis but a case of mania: subinduced
By epilepsy, at the turning-point
Of trance prolonged unduly some three days
When, by the exhibition of some drug
Or spell, exorcisation, stroke of art
Unknown to me and which 'twere well to know,
The evil thing, out-breaking all at once,
Left the man whole and sound of body indeed,—
But, flinging (so to speak) life's gates too wide,
Making a clear house of it too suddenly,
The first conceit that entered might inscribe
Whatever it was minded on the wall
So plainly at that vantage, as it were,
(First come, first served) that nothing subsequent
Attaineth to erase those fancy-scrawls
The just-returned and new-established soul
Hath gotten now so thoroughly by heart
That henceforth she will read or these or none.
And first—the man's own firm conviction rests
That he was dead (in fact they buried him)
—That he was dead and then restored to life
By a Nazarene physician of his tribe:
—'Sayeth, the same bade "Rise," and he did rise,
"Such cases are diurnal," thou wilt cry.

Not so this figment!—not, that such a fume,
Instead of giving way to time and health,
Should eat itself into the life of life.
As saffron tingeth flesh, blood, bones, and all!
For see, how he takes up the after-life,
The man—it is one Lazarus, a Jew,
Sanguine, proportioned, fifty years of age,
The body's habit wholly laudable,
As much, indeed, beyond the common health.
As he were made and put aside to show.
Think, could we penetrate by any drug
And bathe the wearied soul and worried flesh,
And bring it clear and fair, by three days' sleep!
Whence has the man the balm that brightens all?
This grown man eyes the world now like a child.
Some elders of his tribe, I should premise,
Led in their friend, obedient as a sheep,
To bear my inquisition. While they spoke,
Now sharply, now with sorrow,—told the case,—
He listened not except I spoke to him,
But folded his two hands and let them talk,
Watching the flies that buzzed: and yet no fool.
And that's a sample how his years must go.
Look if a beggar, in fixed middle-life,
Should find a treasure,—can he use the same
With straitened habits and with tastes starved small,
And take at once to his impoverished brain
The sudden element that changes things,
That sets the undreamed-of rapture at his hand,

And puts the cheap old joy in the scorned dust?
Is he not such an one as moves to mirth—
Warily parsimonious, when no need,
Wasteful as drunkenness at undue times?
All prudent counsel as to what befits
The golden mean, is lost on such an one:
The man's fantastic will is the man's law.
So here—we call the treasure knowledge, say,
Increased beyond the fleshly faculty—
Heaven opened to a soul while yet on earth,
Earth forced on a soul's use while seeing heaven:
The man is witless of the size, the sum,
The value in proportion of all things,
Or whether it be little or be much.
Discourse to him of prodigious armaments
Assembled to besiege his city now,
And of the passing of a mule with gourds—
'Tis one! Then take it on the other side,
Speak of some trifling fact,—he will gaze rapt
With stupor at its very littleness,
(Far as I see) as if in that indeed
He caught prodigious import, whole results.
And so will turn to us the bystanders
In ever the same stupor (note this point)
That we too see not with his opened eyes.
Wonder and doubt come wrongly into play,
Preposterously, at cross purposes.
Should his child sicken unto death,—why, look
For scarce abatement of his cheerfulness,

Or pretermission of the daily craft!
While a word, gesture, glance from that same child
At play or in the school or laid asleep,
Will startle him to an agony of fear,
Exasperation, just as like. Demand
The reason why—"'tis but a word," object—
"A gesture"—he regards thee as our lord
Who lived there in the pyramid alone,
Looked at us (dost thou mind?) when, being young
We both would unadvisedly recite
Some charm's beginning, from that book of his,
Able to bid the sun throb wide and burst
All into stars, as suns grown old are wont.
Thou and the child have each a veil alike
Thrown o'er your heads, from under which ye both
Stretch your blind hands and trifle with a match
Over a mine of Greek fire, did ye know!
He holds on firmly to some thread of life
(It is the life to lead perforcedly)
Which runs across some vast distracting orb
Of glory on either side that meagre thread,
Which, conscious of, he must not enter yet—
The spiritual life around the earthly life:
The law of that is known to him as this,
His heart and brain move there, his feet stay here.
So is the man perplext with impulses
Sudden to start off crosswise, not straight on,
Proclaiming what is right and wrong across,
And not along, this black thread thro' the blaze—

"It should be" balked by "here it cannot be."
And oft the man's soul springs into his face
As if he saw again and heard again
His sage that bade him "Rise" and he did rise.
Something, a word, a tick o'the blood within
Admonishes: then back he sinks at once
To ashes, who was very fire before,
In sedulous recurrence to his trade
Whereby he earneth him the daily bread;
And studiously the humbler for that pride,
Professedly the faultier that he knows
God's secret, while he holds the thread of life.
Indeed the especial marking of the man
Is prone submission to the heavenly will—
Seeing it, what it is, and why it is.
'Sayeth, he will wait patient to the last
For that same death, which must restore his being
To equilibrium, body loosening soul
Divorced even now by premature full growth:
He will live, nay, it pleaseth him to live
So long as God please, and just how God please.
He even seeketh not to please God more
(Which meaneth, otherwise) than as God please.
Hence, I perceive not he affects to preach
The doctrine of his sect whate'er it be,
Make proselytes as madmen thirst to do:
How can he give his neighbour the real ground,
His own conviction? Ardent as he is—
Call his great truth a lie, why, still the old

"Be it as God please" reassureth him.
I probed the sore as thy disciple should:
"How, beast," said I, "this stolid carelessness
Sufficeth thee, when Rome is on her march
To stamp out like a little spark thy town,
Thy tribe, thy crazy tale and thee at once?"
He merely looked with his large eyes on me,
The man is apathetic, you deduce?
Contrariwise, he loves both old and young,
Able and weak, affects the very brutes
And birds—how say I? flowers of the field—
As a wise workman recognizes tools
In a master's workshop, loving what they make.
Thus is the man as harmless as a lamb:
Only impatient, let him do his best,
At ignorance and carelessness and sin—
An indignation which is promptly curbed:
As when in certain travel I have feigned
To be an ignoramus in our art
According to some preconceived design,
And happed to hear the land's practitioners
Steeped in conceit sublimed by ignorance,
Prattle fantastically on disease,
Its cause and cure—and I must hold my peace!

Thou wilt object—Why have I not ere this
Sought out the sage himself, the Nazarene
Who wrought this cure, inquiring at the source,
Conferring with the frankness that befits?

Alas! it grieveth me, the learned leech
Perished in a tumult many years ago,
Accused—our learning's fate—of wizardry,
Rebellion, to the setting up a rule
And creed prodigious as described to me.
His death, which happened when the earthquake fell
(Prefiguring, as soon appeared, the loss
To occult learning in our lord the sage
Who lived there in the pyramid alone),
Was wrought by the mad people—that's their wont!
On vain recourse, as I conjecture it.
To his tried virtue, for miraculous help—
How could he stop the earthquake? That's their way!
The other imputations must be lies:
But take one, tho' I loathe to give it thee,
In mere respect for any good man's fame.
(And after all, our patient Lazarus
Is stark mad; should we count on what he says?
Perhaps not: tho' in writing to a leech
'Tis well to keep back nothing of a case.)
This man so cured regards the curer, then,
As—God forgive me! who but God Himself,
Creator and sustainer of the world,
That came and dwelt in flesh on it awhile.
—'Sayeth that such an one was born, and lived,
Taught, healed the sick, broke bread at his own house,
Then died; with Lazarus by, for aught I know,
And yet was...what I said nor choose repeat,
And must have so avouched himself, in fact,

In hearing of this very Lazarus
Who saith—but why all this of what he saith?
Why write of trivial matters, things of price
Calling at every moment for remark?
I noticed on the margin of a pool
Blue-flowering borage, the Aleppo sort,
Aboundeth, very nitrous. It is strange!

Thy pardon for this long and tedious case,
Which, now that I review it, needs must seem
Unduly dwelt on, prolixly set forth!
Nor I myself discern in what is writ
Good cause for the peculiar interest
And awe indeed this man has touched me with.
Perhaps the journey's end, the weariness
Had wrought upon me first. I met him thus:
I crossed a ridge of short sharp broken hills
Like an old lion's cheek teeth. Out there came
A moon made like a face with certain spots
Multiform, manifold, and menacing:
Then a wind rose behind me. So we met
In this old sleepy town at unaware,
The man and I. I send thee what is writ.
Regard it as a chance, a matter risked
To this ambiguous Syrian: he may lose,
Or steal, or give it thee with equal good.
Jerusalem's repose shall make amends
For time this letter wastes, thy time and mine;
Till when, once more thy pardon and farewell!

The very God! think, Abib; dost thou think?
So, the All-Great, were the All-Loving too—
So, through the thunder comes a human voice
Saying, "O heart I made, a heart beats here!
Face, my hands fashioned, see it in myself!
Thou hast no power nor mayst conceive of mine,
But love I gave thee, with myself to love,
And thou must love me who have died for thee!"
The madman saith He said so; it is strange.

SAUL

I

Said Abner, "At last thou art come! Ere I tell, ere thou speak.
Kiss my cheek, wish me well!" Then I wished it, and did kiss his cheek.
And he, "Since the King, O my friend, for thy countenance sent,
Neither drunken nor eaten have we; nor until from his tent
Thou return with the joyful assurance the King liveth yet,
Shall our lip with the honey be bright, with the water be wet.
For out of the black mid-tent's silence, a space of three days,
Not a sound hath escaped to thy servants, of prayer nor of praise,
To betoken that Saul and the Spirit have ended their strife,
And that, faint in his triumph, the monarch sinks back upon life.

II

"Yet now my heart leaps, O beloved! God's child with his dew
On thy gracious gold hair, and those lilies still living and blue
Just broken to twine round thy harp-strings, as if no wild heat
Were now raging to torture the desert!"

III

Then I, as was meet,
Knelt down to the God of my fathers, and rose on my feet,
And ran o'er the sand burnt to powder. The tent was unlooped;
I pulled up the spear that obstructed, and under I stooped;

Hands and knees on the slippery grass-patch, all withered and gone,
That extends to the second enclosure. I groped my way on
Till I felt where the foldskirts fly open. Then once more I prayed,
And opened the foldskirts and entered, and was not afraid
But spoke, "Here is David, thy servant!" And no voice replied.
At the first I saw naught but the blackness; but soon I descried
A something more black than the blackness—the vast, the upright
Main prop which sustains the pavilion: and slow into sight
Grew a figure against it, gigantic and blackest of all.
Then a sunbeam, that burst thro' the tent roof, showed Saul.

IV

He stood erect as that tent-prop, both arms stretched out wide
On the great cross-support in the centre, that goes to each side;
He relaxed not a muscle, but hung there as, caught in his pangs
And waiting his change, the king serpent all heavily hangs,
Far away from his kind, in the pine, till deliverance come
With the spring-time,—so agonized Saul, drear and stark, blind and dumb.

V

Then I tuned my harp,—took off the lilies we twine round its chords
Lest they snap 'neath the stress of the noontide—those sunbeams like swords!
And I first played the tune all our sheep know, as, one after one,
So docile they come to the pen-door till folding be done.

They are white and untorn by the bushes, for lo, they have fed
Where the long grasses stifle the water within the stream's bed;
And now one after one seeks its lodging, as star follows star
Into eve and the blue far above us,—so, blue and so far!

VI

—Then the tune, for which quails on the cornland will each leave his mate
To fly after the player; then, what makes the crickets elate
Till for boldness they fight one another: and then, what has weight
To set the quick jerboa a-musing outside his sand house—
There are none such as he for a wonder, half bird and half mouse!
God made all the creatures and gave them our love and our fear,
To give sign, we and they are his children, one family here.

VII

Then I played the help-tune of our reapers, their wine-song, when hand
Grasps at hand, eye lights eye in good friendship, and great hearts expand
And grow one in the sense of this world's life.—And then, the last song
When the dead man is praised on his journey—"Bear, bear him along
With his few faults shut up like dead flowerets!" Are balm-seeds not here
To console us? The land has none left such as he on the bier.
"Oh, would we might keep thee, my brother!"—And then, the glad chaunt
Of the marriage,—first go the young maidens, next, she whom we vaunt
As the beauty, the pride of our dwelling.—And then, the great march

Wherein man runs to man to assist him and buttress an arch

Naught can break; who shall harm them, our friends?—Then, the chorus intoned

As the Levites go up to the altar in glory enthroned.

But I stopped here: for here in the darkness Saul groaned.

VIII

And I paused, held my breath in such silence, and listened apart;

And the tent shook, for mighty Saul shuddered: and sparkles 'gan dart

From the jewels that woke in his turban, at once with a start,

All its lordly male-sapphires, and rubies courageous at heart.

So the head: but the body still moved not, still hung there erect.

And I bent once again to my playing, pursued it unchecked,

As I sang,—

IX

"Oh, our manhood's prime vigor! No spirit feels waste,

Not a muscle is stopped in its playing nor sinew unbraced.

Oh, the wild joys of living! the leaping from rock up to rock,

The strong rending of boughs from the fir-tree, the cool silver shock

Of the plunge in a pool's living water, the hunt of the bear,

And the sultriness showing the lion is couched in his lair.

And the meal, the rich dates yellowed over with gold-dust divine,

And the locust-flesh steeped in the pitcher, the full draught of wine,

And the sleep in the dried river-channel where bulrushes tell

That the water was wont to go warbling so softly and well.

How good is man's life, the mere living! how fit to employ

All the heart and the soul and the senses for ever in joy!
Hast thou loved the white locks of thy father, whose sword thou didst guard
When he trusted thee forth with the armies, for glorious reward?
Didst thou see the thin hands of thy mother, held up as men sung
The low song of the nearly departed, and hear her faint tongue
Joining in while it could to the witness, 'Let one more attest,
I have lived, seen God's hand thro' a lifetime, and all was for best!'
Then they sung thro' their tears in strong triumph, not much, but the rest.
And thy brothers, the help and the contest, the working whence grew
Such result as, from seething grape-bundles, the spirit strained true:
And the friends of thy boyhood—that boyhood of wonder and hope,
Present promise and wealth of the future beyond the eye's scope,—
Till lo, thou art grown to a monarch; a people is thine:
And all gifts which the world offers singly, on one head combine!
On one head, all the beauty and strength, love and rage (like the throe
That, a-work in the rock, helps its labour and lets the gold go),
High ambition and deeds which surpass it, fame crowning them,—all
Brought to blaze on the head of one creature—King Saul!"

X

And lo, with that leap of my spirit,—heart, hand, harp, and voice,
Each lifting Saul's name out of sorrow, each bidding rejoice
Saul's fame in the light it was made for—as when, dare I say,
The Lord's army, in rapture of service, strains thro' its array,
And upsoareth the cherubim-chariot—"Saul!" cried I, and stopped,
And waited the thing that should follow. Then Saul, who hung propped
By the tent's cross-support in the centre, was struck by his name.
Have ye seen when Spring's arrowy summons goes right to the aim,

And some mountain, the last to withstand her, that held (he alone,
While the vale laughed in freedom and flowers) on a broad bust of stone
A year's snow bound about for a breastplate,—leaves grasp of the sheet?
Fold on fold all at once it crowds thunderously down to his feet,
And there fronts you, stark, black, but alive yet, your mountain of old,
With his rents, the successive bequeathings of ages untold:
Yea, each harm got in fighting your battles, each furrow and scar
Of his head thrust 'twixt you and the tempest—all hail, there they are!
—Now again to be softened with verdure, again hold the nest
Of the dove, tempt the goat and its young to the green on his crest
For their food in the ardours of summer. One long shudder thrilled.
All the tent till the very air tingled, then sank and was stilled
At the King's self left standing before me, released and aware.
What was gone, what remained? All to traverse 'twixt hope and despair.
Death was past, life not come; so he waited. Awhile his right hand
Held the brow, helped the eyes left too vacant, forthwith to remand
To their place what new objects should enter: 'twas Saul as before.
I looked up, and dared gaze at those eyes, nor was hurt any more
Than by slow pallid sunsets in autumn, ye watch from the shore,
At their sad level gaze o'er the ocean—a sun's slow decline
Over hills which, resolved in stern silence, o'erlap and entwine
Base with base to knit strength more intensely: so, arm folded arm
O'er the chest whose slow heavings subsided.

XI

What spell or what charm,
(For, awhile there was trouble within me) what next should I urge
To sustain him where song had restored, him? Song filled to the verge
His cup with the wine of this life, pressing all that it yields
Of mere fruitage, the strength and the beauty: beyond, on what fields
Glean a vintage more potent and perfect to brighten the eye,
And bring blood to the lip, and commend them the cup they put by?
He saith, "It is good:" still he drinks not: he lets me praise life,
Gives assent, yet would die for his own part.

XII

Then fancies grew rife
Which had come long ago on the pasture, when round me the sheep
Fed in silence—above, the one eagle wheeled slow as in sleep;
And I lay in my hollow and mused on the world that might lie
'Neath his ken, tho' I saw but the strip 'twixt the hill and the sky:
And I laughed—"Since my days are ordained to be passed with my flocks,
Let me people at least, with my fancies, the plains and the rocks,
Dream the life I am never to mix with, and image the show
Of mankind as they live in those fashions I hardly shall know!
Schemes of life, its best rules and right uses, the courage that gains,
And the prudence that keeps what men strive for!" And now these old trains
Of vague thought came again; I grew surer; so, once more the string
Of my harp made response to my spirit, as thus—

XIII

"Yea, my King,"

I began—"thou dost well in rejecting mere comforts that spring
From the mere mortal life held in common by man and by brute:
In our flesh grows the branch of this life, in our soul it bears fruit.
Thou hast marked the slow rise of the tree,—how its stem trembled first
Till it passed the kid's lip, the stag's antler; then safely outburst
The fan-branches all round; and thou mindest when these too, in turn
Broke a-bloom and the palm-tree seemed perfect: yet more was to learn,
E'en the good that comes in with the palm-fruit. Our dates shall we slight,
When their juice brings a cure for all sorrow? or care for the plight
Of the palm's self whose slow growth produced them? Not so! stem and branch.
Shall decay, nor be known in their place, while the palm-wine shall staunch
Every wound of man's spirit in winter. I pour thee such wine.
Leave the flesh to the fate it was fit for! the spirit be thine!
By the spirit, when age shall o'ercome thee, thou still shalt enjoy
More indeed, than at first when, inconscious, the life of a boy.
Crush that life, and behold its wine running! Each deed thou hast done
Dies, revives, goes to work in the world; until e'en as the sun
Looking down on the earth, tho' clouds spoil him, tho' tempests efface,
Can find nothing his own deed produced not, must everywhere trace
The results of his past summer-prime,—so, each ray of thy will.
Every flash of thy passion and prowess, long over, shall thrill
Thy whole people, the countless, with ardour, till they too give forth
A like cheer to their sons: who in turn, fill the South and the North
With the radiance thy deed was the germ of. Carouse in the past!
But the license of age has its limit; thou diest at last.

As the lion, when age dims his eyeball, the rose at her height,
So with man—so his power and his beauty forever take flight.
No! Again a long draught of my soul-wine! Look forth o'er the years!
Thou hast done now with eyes for the actual; begin with the seer's!
Is Saul dead? In the depth of the vale make his tomb—bid arise
A gray mountain of marble heaped four-square, till, built to the skies,
Let it mark where the great First King slumbers: whose fame would ye know?
Up above see the rock's naked face, where the record shall go
In great characters cut by the scribe,—Such was Saul, so he did;
With the sages directing the work, by the populace chid,—
For not half, they'll affirm, is comprised there! Which fault to amend,
In the grove with his kind grows the cedar, whereon they shall spend
(See, in tablets 'tis level before them) their praise, and record
With the gold of the graver, Saul's story,—the statesman's great word.
Side by side with the poet's sweet comment. The river's a-wave
With smooth paper-reeds grazing each other when prophet-winds rave;
So the pen gives unborn generations their due and their part
In thy being! Then, first of the mighty, thank God that thou art!"

XIV

And behold while I sang...but O Thou who didst grant me that day,
And before it not seldom had granted Thy help to essay.
Carry on and complete an adventure,—my shield and my sword
In that act where my soul was Thy servant, Thy word was my word,—
Still be with me, who then at the summit of human endeavour
And scaling the highest, man's thought could, gazed hopeless as ever
On the new stretch of heaven above me—till, mighty to save,

Just one lift of Thy hand cleared that distance—God's throne from man's grave!

Let me tell out my tale to its ending—my voice to my heart
Which can scarce dare believe in what marvels last night I took part,
As this morning I gather the fragments, alone with my sheep,
And still fear lest the terrible glory evanish like sleep!
For I wake in the gray dewy covert, while Hebron, upheaves
The dawn struggling with night on his shoulder, and Kidron retrieves
Slow the damage of yesterday's sunshine.

XV

I say then,—my song
While I sang thus, assuring the monarch, and, ever more strong,
Made a proffer of good to console him—he slowly resumed.
His old motions and habitudes kingly. The right hand replumed
His black locks to their wonted composure, adjusted the swathes
Of his turban, and see—the huge sweat that his countenance bathes,
He wipes off with the robe; and he girds now his loins as of yore,
And feels slow for the armlets of price, with the clasp set before,
He is Saul, ye remember in glory,—ere error had bent
The broad brow from the daily communion; and still, tho' much spent
Be the life and bearing that front you, the same, God did choose,
To receive what a man may waste, desecrate, never quite lose.
So sank he along by the tent-prop, till, stayed by the pile
Of his armour and war-cloak and garments, he leaned there awhile,
And sat out my singing,—one arm round the tent-prop, to raise
His bent head, and the other hung slack—till I touched on the praise
I foresaw from all men in all time, to the man patient there;

And thus ended, the harp falling forward. Then first I was 'ware
That he sat, as I say, with my head just above his vast knees
Which were thrust out each side around me, like oak roots which please
To encircle a lamb when it slumbers. I looked up to know
If the best I could do had brought solace: he spoke not, but slow
Lifted up the hand slack at his side, till he laid it with care
Soft and grave, but in mild settled will, on my brow: thro' my hair
The large fingers were pushed, and he bent back my head, with kind power—
All my face back, intent to peruse it, as men do a flower.
Thus held he me there with his great eyes that scrutinized mine—
And oh, all my heart how it loved him! but where was the sign?
I yearned—"Could I help thee, my father, inventing a bliss,
I would add, to that life of the past, both the future and this;
I would give thee new life altogether, as good, ages hence.
As this moment,—had love but the warrant, love's heart to dispense!"

XVI

Then the truth came upon me. No harp more—no song more! outbroke—

XVII

"I have gone the whole round of creation: I saw and I spoke;
I, a work of God's hand for that purpose, received in my brain
And pronounced on the rest of his handwork—returned him again
His creation's approval or censure: I spoke as I saw,
Reported, as man may of God's work—all's love, yet all's law.
Now I lay down the judgeship he lent me. Each faculty tasked

To perceive him has gained an abyss, where a dewdrop was asked.
Have I knowledge? confounded it shrivels at Wisdom laid bare.
Have I forethought? how purblind, how blank, to the Infinite Care!
Do I task any faculty highest, to image success?
I but open my eyes,—and perfection, no more and no less,
In the kind I imagined, full-fronts me, and God is seen God
In the star, in the stone, in the flesh, in the soul and the clod.
And thus looking within and around me, I ever renew
(With that stoop of the soul which in bending upraises it too)
The submission of man's nothing-perfect to God's all complete,
As by each new obeisance in spirit, I climb to His feet.
Yet with all this abounding experience, this deity known,
I shall dare to discover some province, some gift of my own,
There's a faculty pleasant to exercise, hard to hoodwink,
I am fain to keep still in abeyance (I laugh as I think),
Lest, insisting to claim and parade in it, wot ye, I worst
E'en the Giver in one gift.—Behold, I could love if I durst!
But I sink the pretension as fearing a man may o'ertake
God's own speed in the one way of love; I abstain for love's sake.
—What, my soul? see thus far and no farther? when doors great and small,
Nine-and-ninety flew ope at our touch; should the hundredth appal?
In the least things have faith, yet distrust in the greatest of all?
Do I find love so full in my nature, God's ultimate gift,
That I doubt His own love can compete with it? Here, the parts shift?
Here, the creature surpass the creator,—the end, what began?
Would I fain in my impotent yearning do all for this man,
And dare doubt He alone shall not help him, who yet alone can?
Would it ever have entered my mind, the bare will, much less power,
To bestow on this Saul what I sang of, the marvellous dower

Of the life he was gifted and filled with? to make such a soul,
Such a body, and then such an earth for insphering the whole?
And doth it not enter my mind (as my warm tears attest),
These good things being given, to go on, and give one more, the best?
Ay, to save and redeem and restore him, maintain at the height
This perfection,—succeed with life's dayspring, death's minute of night?
Interpose at the difficult minute, snatch Saul the mistake,
Saul the failure, the ruin he seems now,—and bid him awake
From the dream, the probation, the prelude, to find himself set
Clear and safe in new light and new life,—a new harmony yet
To be run and continued, and ended—who knows?—or endure!
The man taught enough by life's dream, of the rest to make sure;
By the pain-throb, triumphantly winning intensified bliss,
And the next world's reward and repose, by the struggles in this.

XVIII

"I believe it! 'Tis Thou, God, that givest, 'tis I who receive;
In the first is the last, in Thy will is my power to believe.
All's one gift: Thou canst grant it, moreover, as prompt to my prayer,
As I breathe out this breath, as I open these arms to the air.
From Thy will stream the worlds, life and nature, Thy dread Sabaoth:
I will?—the mere atoms despise me! Why am I not loath
To look that, even that in the face too? Why is it I dare
Think but lightly of such impuissance? What stops my despair?
This;—'tis not what man Does which exalts him, but what man Would do!
See the King—I would help him, but cannot, the wishes fall through.
Could I wrestle to raise him from sorrow, grow poor to enrich,
To fill up his life, starve my own out, I would—knowing which,

I know that my service is perfect. Oh, speak thro' me now!
Would I suffer for him that I love? So wouldst Thou—so wilt Thou!
So shall crown Thee the topmost, ineffablest, uttermost crown—
And Thy love fill infinitude wholly, nor leave up nor down
One spot for the creature to stand in! It is by no breath,
Turn of eye, wave of hand, that salvation joins issue with death!
As Thy love is discovered almighty, almighty be proved
Thy power, that exists with and for it, of being Beloved!
He who did most, shall bear most; the strongest shall stand the most weak,
'Tis the weakness in strength, that I cry for! my flesh, that I seek
In the Godhead! I seek and I find it, O Saul, it shall be
A Face like my face that receives thee: a Man like to me,
Thou shalt love and be loved by, forever: a Hand like this hand
Shall throw open the gates of new life to thee! See the Christ stand!"

XIX

I know not too well how I found my way home in the night.
There were witnesses, cohorts about me, to left and to right,
Angels, powers, the unuttered, unseen, the alive, the aware:
I repressed, I got thro' them as hardly, as stragglingly there,
As a runner beset by the populace famished for news—
Life or death. The whole earth was awakened, hell loosed with her crews;
And the stars of night beat with emotion, and tingled and shot
Out in fire the strong pain of pent knowledge: but I fainted not,
For the Hand still impelled me at once and supported, suppressed
All the tumult, and quenched it with quiet, and holy behest,
Till the rapture was shut in itself, and the earth sank to rest.
Anon at the dawn, all that trouble had withered from earth—

Not so much, but I saw it die out in the day's tender birth;
In the gathered intensity brought to the gray of the hills;
In the shuddering forests' held breath; in the sudden wind-thrills;
In the startled wild beasts that bore off, each with eye sidling still
Though averted with wonder and dread; in the birds stiff and chill
That rose heavily, as I approached them, made stupid with awe:
E'en the serpent that slid away silent—he felt the new law.
The same stared in the white humid faces upturned by the flowers;
The same worked in the heart of the cedar and moved the vine-bowers;
And the little brooks witnessing murmured, persistent and low.
With their obstinate, all but hushed voices—"E'en so, it is so!"

ONE WORD MORE

TO E.B.B.

(Epilogue to 'Men and Women')

I

There they are, my fifty men and women
Naming me the fifty poems finished!
Take them, Love, the book and me together;
Where the heart lies, let the brain lie also.

II

Rafael made a century of sonnets,
Made and wrote them in a certain volume
Dinted with the silver-pointed pencil
Else he only used to draw Madonnas;
These, the world might view—but one, the volume.
Who that one, you ask? Your heart instructs you.
Did she live and love it all her lifetime?
Did she drop, his lady of the sonnets,
Die, and let it drop beside her pillow
Where it lay in place of Rafael's glory,
Rafael's cheek so duteous and so loving—
Cheek, the world was wont to hail a painter's,
Rafael's cheek, her love had turned a poet's?

III

You and I would rather read that volume
(Taken to his beating bosom by it),
Lean and list the bosom-beats of Rafael,
Would we not? than wonder at Madonnas—
Her, San Sisto names, and Her, Foligno,
Her, that visits Florence in a vision,
Her, that's left with lilies in the Louvre—
Seen by us and all the world in circle.

IV

You and I will never read that volume.
Guido Reni, like his own eye's apple,
Guarded long the treasure-book and loved it.
Guido Reni dying, all Bologna
Cried, and the world cried too, "Ours, the treasure!"
Suddenly, as rare things will, it vanished.

V

Dante once prepared to paint an angel:
Whom to please? You whisper "Beatrice."
While he mused and traced it and retraced it
(Peradventure with a pen corroded
Still by drops of that hot ink he dipped for,
When, his left-hand i'the hair o'the wicked,
Back he held the brow and pricked its stigma,

Bit into the live man's flesh for parchment,
Loosed him, laughed to see the writing rankle,
Let the wretch go festering through Florence)—
Dante, who loved well because he hated,
Hated wickedness that hinders loving,
Dante, standing, studying his angel,—
In there broke the folk of his Inferno.
Says he—"Certain people of importance"
(Such he gave his daily dreadful line to)
"Entered and would seize, forsooth, the poet."
Says the poet—"Then I stopped my painting."

VI

You and I would rather see that angel,
Painted by the tenderness of Dante,
Would we not?—than read a fresh Inferno.

VII

You and I will never see that picture.
While he mused on love and Beatrice,
While he softened o'er his outlined angel,
In they broke, those "people of importance":
We and Bice bear the loss forever.

VIII

What of Rafael's sonnets, Dante's picture?
This: no artist lives and loves, that longs not
Once, and only once, and for one only,
(Ah, the prize!) to find his love a language
Fit and fair and simple and sufficient—
Using nature that's an art to others,
Not, this one time, art that's turned his nature.
Ay, of all the artists living, loving,
None but would forego his proper dowry,—
Does he paint? he fain would write a poem,
Does he write? he fain would paint a picture,—
Put to proof art alien to the artist's,
Once, and only once, and for one only,
So to be the man and leave the artist,
Gain the man's joy, miss the artist's sorrow.

IX

Wherefore? Heaven's gift takes earth's abatement!
He who smites the rock and spreads the water,
Bidding drink and live a crowd beneath him,
Even he, the minute makes immortal,
Proves, perchance, but mortal in the minute,
Desecrates, belike, the deed in doing.
While he smites, how can he but remember,
So he smote before, in such a peril,
When they stood and mocked—"Shall smiting help us?"

When they drank and sneered—"A stroke is easy!"
When they wiped their mouths and went their journey,
Throwing him for thanks—"But drought was pleasant."
Thus old memories mar the actual triumph;
Thus the doing savors of disrelish;
Thus achievement lacks a gracious somewhat;
O'er-importuned brows becloud the mandate,
Carelessness or consciousness—the gesture.
For he bears an ancient wrong about him,
Sees and knows again those phalanxed faces,
Hears, yet one time more, the 'customed prelude—
"How shouldst thou, of all men, smite, and save us?"
Guesses what is like to prove the sequel—
"Egypt's flesh-pots—nay, the drought was better."

X

Oh, the crowd must have emphatic warrant!
Theirs, the Sinai-forehead's cloven brilliance,
Right-arm's rod-sweep, tongue's imperial fiat.
Never dares the man put off the prophet.

XI

Did he love one face from out the thousands,
(Were she Jethro's daughter, white and wifely,
Were she but the Æthiopian bondslave),
He would envy yon dumb, patient camel,
Keeping a reserve of scanty water

Meant to save his own life in the desert;
Ready in the desert to deliver
(Kneeling down to let his breast be opened)
Hoard and life together for his mistress.

XII

I shall never, in the years remaining,
Paint you pictures, no, nor carve you statues.
Make you music that should all-express me;
So it seems; I stand on my attainment.
This of verse alone, one life allows me;
Verse and nothing else have I to give you;
Other heights in other lives, God willing;
All the gifts from all the heights, your own, Love.

XIII

Yet a semblance of resource avails us—
Shade so finely touched, love's sense must seize it.
Take these lines, look lovingly and nearly,
Lines I write the first time and the last time.
He who works in fresco steals a hair-brush,
Curbs the liberal hand, subservient proudly,
Cramps his spirit, crowds its all in little,
Makes a strange art of an art familiar,

Fills his lady's missal-marge with flowerets,
He who blows through bronze may breathe through silver,
Fitly serenade a slumbrous princess.
He who writes, may write for once as I do.

XIV

Love, you saw me gather men and women,
Live or dead or fashioned by my fancy,
Enter each and all, and use their service,
Speak from every mouth,—the speech, a poem.
Hardly shall I tell my joys and sorrows,
Hopes and fears, belief and disbelieving:
I am mine and yours—the rest be all men's,
Karshish, Cleon, Norbert, and the fifty.
Let me speak this once in my true person,
Not as Lippo, Roland, or Andrea,
Though the fruit of speech be just this sentence:
Pray you, look on these my men and women,
Take and keep my fifty poems finished;
Where my heart lies, let my brain lie also!
Poor the speech; be how I speak, for all things.

XV

Not but that you know me! Lo, the moon's self!
Here in London, yonder late in Florence,
Still we find her face, the thrice-transfigured.
Curving on a sky imbrued with color,

Drifted over Fiesole by twilight,
Came she, our new crescent of a hair's-breadth.
Full she flared it, lamping Samminiato,
Rounder 'twixt the cypresses and rounder,
Perfect till the nightingales applauded.
Now, a piece of her old self, impoverished,
Hard to greet, she traverses the house-roofs,
Hurries with unhandsome thrift of silver,
Goes dispiritedly, glad to finish.

XVI

What, there's nothing in the moon noteworthy?
Nay: for if that moon could love a mortal,
Use, to charm him (so to fit a fancy),
All her magic ('tis the old sweet mythos),
She would turn a new side to her mortal,
Side unseen of herdsman, huntsman, steersman,—
Blank to Zoroaster on his terrace,
Blind to Galileo on his turret.
Dumb to Homer, dumb to Keats—him, even!
Think, the wonder of the moonstruck mortal—
When she turns round, comes again in heaven,
Opens out anew for worse or better!
Proves she like some portent of an iceberg
Swimming full upon the ship it founders,
Hungry with huge teeth of splintered crystals?
Proves she as the paved work of a sapphire,
Seen by Moses when he climbed the mountain?

Moses, Aaron, Nadab, and Abihu
Climbed and saw the very God, the Highest,
Stand upon the paved work of a sapphire.
Like the bodied heaven in his clearness
Shone the stone, the sapphire of that paved work,
When they ate and drank and saw God also!

XVII

What were seen? None knows, none ever will know.
Only this is sure—the sight were other,
Not the moon's same side, born late in Florence,
Dying now impoverished here in London.
God be thanked, the meanest of his creatures
Boasts two soul-sides, one to face the world with,
One to show a woman when he loves her.

XVIII

This I say of me, but think of you, Love!
This to you—yourself my moon of poets!
Ah, but that's the world's side, there's the wonder,
Thus they see you, praise you, think they know you!
There, in turn I stand with them and praise you—
Out of my own self, I dare to phrase it.
But the best is when I glide from out them,

Cross a step or two of dubious twilight,
Come out on the other side, the novel
Silent silver lights and darks undreamed of,
Where I hush and bless myself with silence.

XIX

Oh, their Rafael of the dear Madonnas,
Oh, their Dante of the dread Inferno,
Wrote one song—and in my brain I sing it,
Drew one angel—borne, see, on my bosom!